Praise for

I Am Rembrandt's Daughter

An ALA Best Book for Young Adults

★ "Cullen's novel is noteworthy for its emotional depth and sensitive development of characters. . . . Cullen creates a powerful family drama." —*Booklist*, starred review

"Readers . . . will cheer for this colorful cast, especially the likable heroine and the understanding and peace she crafts with her father." —*Publishers Weekly*

"Historical fiction, mystery, and romance are masterfully woven, . . . enchanting readers to remain for just another chapter, and then more." —*VOYA*

"[An] absorbing, well-told story." —*SLJ*

"Lynn Cullen has woven carefully researched facts together with imaginative page-turning scenes to create a beautiful story. . . . A wonderful book." —Teenreads.com

I Am Rembrandt's Daughter

I Am Rembrandt's Daughter

LYNN CULLEN

NEW YORK • BERLIN • LONDON

First published by Bloomsbury U.S.A. Children's Books in 2007
Paperback edition published in 2008

Published by Bloomsbury U.S.A. Children's Books
175 Fifth Avenue, New York, New York 10010

The Library of Congress has cataloged the hardcover edition as follows:
Cullen, Lynn.
I am Rembrandt's daughter / by Lynn Cullen.—1st U.S. ed.
p. cm.
Summary: In Amsterdam in the mid-1600s, Cornelia's life as the illegitimate child of renowned painter Rembrandt is marked by plague, poverty, and despair at ever earning her father's love, until she sees hope for a better future in the eyes of a wealthy suitor.
ISBN-13: 978-1-59990-046-9 • ISBN-10: 1-59990-046-7 (hardcover)
[1. Fathers and daughters—Fiction. 2. Rembrandt Harmenszoon van Rijn, 1606–1669—Fiction. 3. Painters—Fiction. 4. Plague—Fiction. 5. Poverty—Fiction. 6. Netherlands—History—17th century—Fiction.] I. Title.
PZ7.C8963Iaam 2007 [Fic]—dc22 2006028197

ISBN-13: 978-1-59990-294-4 • ISBN-10: 1-59990-294-X (paperback)

Typeset by Westchester Book Composition
Printed in the U.S.A. by Quebecor World Fairfield
1 3 5 7 9 10 8 6 4 2

For Mike
My partner on the road trips to Amsterdam,
and in life.

19 May
Anno 1670
Amsterdam

All those years living across the canal from the New Maze Park, and I never did make it inside. In spite of the promises I pried from my moeder, *I never did get a taste of the pancakes frying in hot butter that I could smell from our porch step where I went to escape my* vader's *shouting. I never did get to chase the blue-bellied peacocks whose squawks, even from this side of the hedges and across the murky green water of the canal, pierced so many of my moeder's silences. I never did get to run my hands through the water of the fountains I could hear splashing inside the park when I was sent to fetch my vader, too long at the tavern. But it is too late now. I am new-wed and our ship leaves for the East Indies in a fortnight, and there are accounts to settle.*

Behind me two men paw over my vader's things. They think that because I stand at the open studio window and point myself in the direction of the park, I don't hear or see them. A girl of sixteen, plainly dressed, is invisible to bargain hunters.

"Couldn't get a sword through this." The taller man, the one in the black wool doublet that is short in the sleeves and shiny with wear across the shoulders, pokes a bony finger through the rusty eye slit of an antique helmet. His long neck takes a dip at his Adam's apple, which, combined with the thistledown knot of hair on the top of his head and the feathery white tufts of his brows, gives him the look of a new-hatched stork. "I can barely fit my finger through it."

"Let me see." The other man takes the helmet from the first man's hands. "Damage to the nosepiece. Ruins its value," he says, though he doesn't put it down. He is short limbed and plump and wears the longest, most beautifully ironed white linen collar I have ever seen. It would have looked elegant on a man twice his size, but on him, it resembles an infant's bib. His fat cheeks and puffy lips only add to the effect, giving him the appearance of a large spoiled baby.

"Who was that French king who died from a lance poked through the eyehole of his helmet?" says the big baby. "About a hundred years ago?"

The Stork shrugs.

"Henri the Second," Big Baby says, answering his own question.

"That sounds right."

"I know it is." Big Baby purses his lips as he puts down the helmet. "They don't make things like they used to. Everything is from the Indies these days, not your solid Dutch manufacturing."

The wide wooden floorboards creak under their feet as they move on to examine the next set of shelves.

Big Baby sneezes. "So dusty up here."

"The old fellow hasn't been around here for a while."

"Well, so far I don't see anything worth making an offer on, just a lot of rubbish. What is that?"

The Stork turns a tall, fluid-filled jar in which pink ropes and pale, almost see-through strips of matter swirl like seaweed around a spongy white stick. Big Baby peers at it closely, dabbing his nose with a lacy handkerchief.

"I do believe... Good heavens, it's an arm! Look—see the fingers?"

"Ja, I do now."

"A flayed arm. I'd heard old Rembrandt was a student of anatomy. He must have used this to help him paint musculature."

"I suppose he did."

"I know he did. He would have needed the help, wouldn't he? Lost his grip in his latter years, I would say."

The men linger over the jar and the three others like it, then shuffle on to the row of unframed paintings propped against one wall. They pass without a second look at a painting of a maid shading a candle with her hand, a canvas of two African men, and one of a young man in tatters, kneeling before a bearded gentleman.

"Too dark," Big Baby mutters under his breath. "And much, much too rough. You can see every stroke! Imagine—he used to be the greatest painter in Amsterdam. Now I wouldn't give six stuivers *for the lot."*

I resist the urge to tell them to leave and remind myself that the battle is over. Let it be. I have a husband to think about now. Let the past stay in the past. I close my eyes and let the damp Amsterdam breeze blowing in through the window cool my face.

"I'd heard of him," says the Stork, "when I was a boy."

"We all did."

They pause before the next canvas, which is so covered with splotches of red, brown, and golden paint, that from this angle, it has the choppy surface of a canal in the rain. Big Baby starts to waddle away, then stops when his tall friend won't move.

"What?"

The Stork keeps looking. "There's something about this..."

It is difficult enough to watch them pick through Vader's things, but for strangers to stare at this particular painting...

"Don't look too close," I say. "The smell of paint will not agree with you."

The Stork startles, then notices me by the window. Big Baby looks at me, too, then frowns as he sniffs at the painting. "There's no smell to this. It can't have been wet for at least a year, not if it's a real Rembrandt. I doubt if it is—it's rough, even for him." He tips his head toward me, then under his breath, says to the Stork, "Who's the girl?"

"Rembrandt's maid?" the Stork whispers.

I smile to myself as I turn back to the window. Close. But not quite.

"Where is your master?" Big Baby says loudly. "I'd like to offer him a guilder for this picture."

A single guilder, when Vader's paintings used to fetch thousands from princes. A paltry guilder for this, of all pictures. Gravediggers get twenty for their services, as well I know. Well, I don't care if we need the money for our journey.

"It's not for sale."

"What'd she say?" Big Baby asks his companion, as if I spoke in some sort of incomprehensible maid tongue.

"She said it's not for sale," says the Stork.

"I don't see how this girl would have the authority to make such a decision," Big Baby says. "But no matter. Who wants such a messy old thing, anyhow?"

With another crunch of the floorboards, they move on to a stuffed bird of paradise and Vader's collection of shells. I cannot help but return my gaze to the canvas, with its blaze of reds and golds and comforting browns. How well I know this painting. Many times I have examined it up close and wondered how Vader could make an arrangement of brushstrokes so neatly add up to everything that is important to me. Now, across the studio, I can see neither the short jots nor long swaths of paint. They have melted together to form a scene more dear to me than anything in the world. It is more than just canvas and primer and pigments mixed in oil. Like so many other of Vader's paintings, it is the story of my life.

Chapter 1

Three years earlier . . .

Two girls about my age–nearly fourteen–walk arm in arm down the frost-etched bricks of the sidewalk on the other side of the canal. Even from this side of the window, when the wind gusts, I fancy I can hear the rustle of their fine silk dresses under their fur-trimmed capes as they pass the locked gates of the New Maze Park. An older woman in thick furs waddles behind them like a huge glossy beaver, her proud gaze set on their backs. She must be their moeder.

Brats.

From upstairs, Vader shouts, "TITUS!"

My old cat, Tijger, shifts on my lap, setting off a fresh round of rusty purring. In the summer, with the windows open, you can hear the wheezy organ music and the strangled shrieks of peacocks coming from the park. You can catch the distant shouts of vendors selling pancakes and pickled herring to people lucky enough to have a few spare stuivers jingling in their pockets. Now, in late December, all is quiet in the park.

"TITUS! YOU WASTE TIME!"

With a sigh, I mark my place in my book with a scrap of cloth, then put Tijger from my lap and brush off my apron. Tijger follows me slowly up the stairs, swaying like royalty. He is more than nine years of age—young for people but old enough in cat time. After Titus and my books, he is my closest friend.

Up in my vader's workshop, the cooing of wood doves comes from outside the window near where Vader stands at an easel. On the shelves around him are ancient helmets, stuffed birds from New Guinea, and dusty seashells. There are swords and pole axes all in a jumble and a straw mannequin with its hand twisted into a wave. My favorite items are the four jars each containing its own flayed human arm. Charming. And Titus asks why I never have any of the neighborhood girls over for a visit.

Vader glances at me. "Oh. Cornelia." He always carries his voice low in his throat, as if his words have to fight him before he will let them out. "Where is Titus?"

I go over and jab at the remains of the peat sod smoldering in the fireplace. Vader will let the fire go out, then he'll shout as if attacked by cutpurses for someone to come relight it. Me.

"He's out," I say. "Trying to make money."

If Vader takes the hint, he does not show it. His voice thunders up from deep in his barrel of a chest. "Tell me how this looks."

Once the fire is gnawing at the peat with a hushed and satisfying crackle, I pick up Tijger and peer over Vader's shoulder. The oily smell of his paint makes my head hurt though I should be used to it. Paint stink has filled my nose since I lay in my hand-me-down cradle. Now Vader dabs more paint on a canvas already shingled with thousands of little slabs of it. No smooth, glossy surfaces for my vader, though even I, an ignorant girl, know that rough painting, with every brushstroke showing, is unsellable. No rich merchant from the East India Company wants a splotchy mess on the wall of his mansion on the Prince's Canal, yet here is Vader, working on a choppy picture of a family with two smiling parents and their three happy children. I laugh. What does Vader know about happy families?

Vader crooks a corner of his thin lips, which are as red as a child's, even though the rest of his face is flabby and yellowing. He was old when I was born, though my mother was twenty-eight. "What is the jest?"

Tijger fights to get down. I set him on the floor. "Nothing. Who were your models? You've had no families up here lately."

When Vader doesn't answer, I go to the rear window. Doves scuttle to one side of the ledge as I look through the thick panes against which thorny naked rose vines rattle. A deep *bong* rocks the sill on which I lean, giving me a start. It is the death bells of the West Church, at the end of our canal. It has been four years since that terrible time of plague, and still the Westerkerk's foul bells make me flinch. How does one get over a time such as that? In the final year of the pestilence, twenty thousand people died, one for every ten in the city. The death bells had sounded day and night. Funeral processions lined up at the churchyard gates, waiting their turn to bury the victims from the families able to scrape together the guilders for a funeral and the gravedigger. The other choice was to toss a body into the pit behind the Plague Hospital and sprinkle it with quicklime. No street in the city had been without a house whose occupants were locked behind a door marked with a hastily painted *P* for *pest*, and our street—our house—had been no different.

Now, on the other side of our bare patch of courtyard, two of the van Roop girls jump ropes outside their back door. Their family is new-come to the neighborhood. The family who had lived there before them, the Bickers, had all been taken by the sickness and no one would rent the house for years. Now the van Roop moeder, her bundled baby on her hip, pulls wash off the clothesline strung across the back of the house. All of a sudden I know who Vader is painting.

"It's the van Roops—they are the family on your canvas."

Vader throws a grin over his shoulder.

I fight off a wave of pride for having guessed correctly. Cleverness buys no bread. But at least now it makes sense. For weeks I had noticed Vader staring out the back window of his studio when I had brought him his tray for dinner. When I told Titus about it some days ago at breakfast, he merely dunked his bread in his watery ale and said, "So?"

I had voiced what everyone whispers in Amsterdam. "So the old man is going mad."

"You are just learning this?"

"Well, I think he has gotten worse."

"Maybe," Titus said around a mouthful of bread. Only Titus, with his smooth dark brows, dimpled chin, and finely cut lips, can manage to look handsome while loading his cheeks with half a loaf. Perhaps it is the way his coppery hair curls to his shoulders. My hair is a darker red-brown, with waves given to frizz when it rains. And while his eyes are a hundred interesting shades of green arranged in a halo of flecks, mine are the plain brown of a cow's. It is obvious we have different mothers.

My own chunk of bread crumbled into my ale. I fished the soggy bit from the bottom of my mug. "How can you be so calm? We can't even pay the baker's bill."

"Things may change."

Hope rose in me like a soap bubble. "Have you had luck with the prints?" Titus had been making the rounds of dealers lately with some prints Vader had made several years ago. Usually there is a market for Vader's etchings. If only we could get him to stop his crazy painting and make more of them.

"With the prints?" Titus said as he sliced another piece of cheese. "No, not just yet."

"Why doesn't he give people what they want?" I cried. "Vader can paint as smoothly as anyone—I have seen his old pictures. Why does he have to throw globs of paint on the canvas like dog mess?"

Titus gave me a pitying look. "You are as stubborn as he is. Once you figure out that you cannot change him, you will feel so much better." He wiped his mouth, then pushed back his bench.

"Don't you care what happens to us?"

Titus bared his teeth at his reflection in the kitchen window. "Yes."

"Where are you going?" I hoped I did not know the answer though I was certain that I did. He was always running off to the van Loos' fancy house on the Singel, to see Magdalena. As if he had a chance with her. "Don't go."

His expression was that of an amused angel. "Why, my little Worry Bird?"

He was shaming himself, chasing her so, that was why. The van Loos would never have him, poor as we are. The son of an out-of-fashion painter would make a terrible match for someone of their sort, though Titus's mother, Saskia—who was not my mother, as even strangers will so kindly point out—was the van Loos' cousin. Saskia had married Vader when he was the most promising young artist in Amsterdam. Now that Vader was a broken old man, the van Loos could not possibly wish to taint their line with the likes of us. Not with me in the family, the daughter of Rembrandt by his housemaid.

And anyhow, if Titus married Magdalena, I would die of loneliness.

"Just stay," I said.

"I've got work to do," said Titus.

Only Titus's willingness to knock on dealers' doors has kept us out of the poorhouse. No dealer wants to speak to Vader. They cannot sell the strange work that he does, and besides, he owes them all money. I had hugged my arms to my chest as Titus plunked his hat over his coppery curls and left.

Now, in Vader's dusty studio, Tijger rubs against my legs, wanting to be picked up again now that I have put him down. I obey. He weighs less than he used to, as if age were hollowing his bones.

"What are you going to do with this picture?" I ask Vader. Maybe a patron with money has come to him directly and asked him to portray a family. It is possible. Vader does receive a commission now and then, and sometimes, miraculously, it pleases him to please a patron.

"Do with it?" Vader asks in his guttural voice.

"Did someone ask you for it?"

"Yes." He dabs the finest point of white in the mother's eye. The sound of cooing doves echoes in the room. "God."

Something shrivels inside of me. No one else's vader speaks of God as if he actually knew Him. Normal vaders keep God where He belongs, in church. Vader doesn't even go to church, and he got Moeder kicked out of it when he wouldn't marry her after I was born. He heaps shame upon himself and his family, yet seems to chat as freely to God as did Moses in the Bible, without the bother of the burning bush. "I should get dinner," I murmur.

I go back downstairs, Tijger trailing me majestically, fetch my book, then go to check on the pot of cabbage, onions, and a soupbone I had put upon the kitchen fire. There will be enough soup for Titus if he will come home for supper, but there is no guarantee of that. Each day Titus is gone longer trying to sell Vader's work when he is not falling over himself at Magdalena's. I am here with just Vader and his best friend, God Almighty, unless Neel comes.

The very thought of Cornelis Suythof—Neel, as he has us call him—makes me squirm. Once Vader had many pupils, Titus tells me, before we lost the big house and took this cheap place by the canal. I can still hear the sound of students tramping up the wide stairs of our grand old house, laughing, singing naughty songs, dropping their brushes or palettes with a clatter. Only a few pupils followed Vader to our new house, and now Vader has but one—Neel the Serious, with his messy dark hair and staring eyes. If only he smiled now and then, he would be handsome in a dark and even manly way, but at twenty-one, when he should be dashing and merry like Titus, he is as somber as a church tower.

I am on my stool, my book open on my lap, when footsteps tap outside the open window. Someone bounds from the street onto our stoop; the front door creaks open. The footsteps head not to the studio, but my way. It is too early for Titus. Oh,

Lord, Serious Neel is due for lessons. What does he want from me now?

But it is Titus who trots into the kitchen and picks up the ladle in the pot over the fire. "Cabbage again, milady?"

It is odd how relief stings more than anger. "Don't speak ill of it unless you cook it yourself."

"Why, little Worry Bird, what is the matter? If it's cabbage that's making you cranky, you'll be happy to hear that soon you will not have to dine on a steady diet of it—not if I can help it."

"You sold some prints!" I jump up. My book slides to the floor.

He grins when he picks up the book. "*The Seven Deadly Sins of Maidservants*? The things you read. Weren't you reading *Famous Courtesans* last week?"

I snatch the book from his hands. "Who'd you sell the prints to? Tell me they fetched at least a guilder. We need to pay the baker and the greengrocer and—"

He grabs me by the arms and gives me a playful shake. "Bird! Hush! Worry, worry, worry, when you should be congratulating me!"

"Why?" I say, my head rattling.

He lets me go. "Your big brother is getting married. Magdalena and I are to wed as soon as the banns are published."

Chapter 2

Peter Denying Christ.

1660. Canvas.

It is afternoon and I am on my knees, pulling a string for Tijger to chase. A flash lights the dark room. Thunder rattles the windowpanes and the pictures on the walls. I am five and big and do not get scared at a silly thing like thunder. I get up on my tiptoes to look outside. Rain is coming down sideways, bouncing off the stones of the street, making little pocks in the water of the canal like the marks in Vader's cheeks. It has beaten the petals off the tulips that grow under our tree. I look behind me. Where is Tijger? Thunder booms again.

I jump up and run to the back room and tag the bed-cupboard where Moeder sleeps.

"Moeder, wake up!"

"Nicolaes," she whispers.

Silly moeder! "No, it's Neeltje."

Moeder's eyes open. Slowly, like she is underwater, she reaches for me. Just before her hand reaches my cheek, it drops. Her eyes slowly close again.

Moeder sleeps a lot. Unless she is cleaning.

I climb up onto the bed and sit in the afternoon dark. I pick my nose until there is nothing left to pick, then try to tie the laces that have come undone on my top. I twist them one way, then another—how do I make a loop?

A skittering sound comes from across the room. The hairs prick on my arms. Last week during the night, I had awoken with a rat on me. When I screamed, Vader barked from his bed above my pallet, "Go back to sleep!"

The rat had sat on my chest, looking at me, twitching its dirty whiskers.

"But… it's a rat!"

Vader grunted something to Moeder, then rustled the bedclothes.

The rat sprang away, its nails poking into my shift.

"All I wanted was sleep!" Vader stepped over my pallet and left the room.

I popped up. "Moeder?"

She held up the top feather bag. I crawled underneath next to her.

"It's almost dawn, pretty puss," she had said in a sleepy voice. "No more rats. Rats hate the light."

Now, in the dark of the stormy afternoon, I hear the rustling again. I crawl up to Moeder's face again.

"Moeder?" When she doesn't answer, I put my eyes up to hers. Still asleep.

There is an unlit lamp across the room, sitting on its shelf in the wall. It's too high for me to reach, and if I could, how would I light it? Even if I were allowed to touch a fireplace, there is only one lit and it is in the kitchen, and who knows how many rats might be hiding between here and there?

I hear a creaking overhead. Vader, in his studio. He would have light.

With all the courage I can muster, I dash up the stairs, then crawl to a corner of Vader's room. Three lamps are eating up the darkness. If I am very quiet, Vader might not see me.

Vader is sketching at his desk, the hanging sleeve of his brown gown waggling from his elbow as he works. He stops and swallows. He sniffs. I hold my breath. His sleeve waggles again.

I stay frozen in my spot as long as I can. But the hard floor hurts my tailbone and my bottom itches because Moeder forgot to dress me in my shift after my bath yesterday and my wool skirt torments my skin. I cannot . . . keep . . . still. Look at how the firelight sputters in the lamp nearest me, the one Vader had put on the floor behind him. As quiet as the sneakiest rat, I crawl to it and put my hand in front of its light. My skin glows red as if lit from within. Inside, there are knotty sticks that run the length of my fingers. I look up at the arm floating in the jar on the shelf. The skin has been peeled back like the petals on a tulip; meaty strings float around the bone. I look at my own hand. There is a whole other being sealed up in there, an ugly one I do not want to know.

"What are you doing?" Vader says.

I jerk my hand behind my back.

"Where is your mother?"

"Asleep."

"Then why do you not go play?"

I look at the rain pouring down outside the window. "I—I'm hungry. I have not had de noen*."*

"No lunch? It's two o'clock. She should get up." Vader frowns. "Never mind, do what you were doing." He nods. "Put your hand in front of the lamp."

I cannot move. Is this a test?

"Go on, Cornelia. Put your hand in front of the lamp like you were doing—but come around to this side and do it."

I hear Moeder's voice in my head, You must never play with fire. *If I make the wrong move, I will be shut out in the dark. I bite my hand.*

"What's wrong with you, girl? How'd I ever raise such a timid thing? Just put your hand in front of the lamp."

The front door scrapes open, slams. Footsteps pound up the stairs.

"What a storm!" Titus wipes his face with his arm.

I see the tracks his wet stockings have left on the wood floor. Moeder won't like that.

"Titus," Vader says, "come here and put your hand in front of this lamp."

Titus raises his brows at me, shrugs, then squats next to me. He holds his hand before the light. "What is wrong?" he whispers to me.

Vader goes back to his desk. "Titus, move your hand to the left."

Titus does what Vader says. He makes a face only I can see as Vader sketches over finished parts of his drawing, his sleeve flapping, flapping.

Vader stops drawing, runs to Titus, and grabs his face. "You!" he says, kissing him on both cheeks. "You gave me the heart of the picture! The light of God shining unto Peter. It shines through the maid, making her hand transparent! Brilliant! Brilliant! Son, what would I do without you?"

Titus laughs.

I crawl back to the corner, forgotten. Better that, than to be shouted at.

Later, when the painting is finished, Moeder tells me it is a picture of St. Peter, at the moment he said he did not know Jesus for the third time. But my care is for the maid in the picture, holding the lamp up to Peter. You can see into her hand, like I had seen into my own. You can see the bones of the secret stranger hiding inside. Why doesn't it bother people that their insides don't match their outsides? It bothers me. I don't sleep that night, afraid that my insides will come crawling out.

Chapter 3

Almost three months have passed since the terrible announcement of Titus's engagement, and now, on this, the most doleful of occasions, Titus's wedding, my own feet betray me. The rotten traitors wish to skip under my good dress. It is the happy call of viol and lute, the whinny of the bagpipe—my stupid feet can hardly resist it. Even as the damp late-February wind nips at my hands and face, my feet want to behave like idiots as we march in the torchlight from the church to the bride's house. No one else dances. All around me I hear the muted patter of soft leather against cobblestone and the somber jingle of gold chains and jeweled belts—the sounds of rich people walking. When the people from our neighborhood march to a wedding feast, they clatter merrily along in their wooden *clompen* and cough.

I look over my shoulder to make sure Vader is not dancing

like a peasant. Miraculously, he is not, though he is grinning like a simpleton. Of course, he's grinning. He has married his son well and now he thinks Titus will help him with expenses. Who gave Titus life? he'll argue. From whom did Titus inherit his irresistible coppery curls? His charming smile? He will not mention Titus's slightly bulbous nose, a neater version of his own spongy affair. At least I did not inherit that.

I squint ahead, seeking out the bride and groom. Magdalena is easy to find—the diamonds in her white-blond hair wink in the bobbing torchlight; the gold cloth collar and cuffs of her garnet robe shine. But it is not this finery that holds my gaze. What does are Titus's long fingers, wrapped around her delicate hand.

My face burns from the cold by the time we reach the Apple Market. On the other side of the market, across the Singel, which reeks of fish, Magdalena's house, called the House of the Gilded Scales, seems to blaze before us, its fire made double by the reflection of the windows on the black water of the canal. They must be burning a fortune in candles in there.

Vader nods at someone as we march over the wooden drawbridge to the house. I look through the crowd and see a wispy young man in a large hat, Gerrit van Uylenburgh, nodding back. I have seen Gerrit van Uylenburgh before, when I have been out with Titus. He is a well-known art dealer in Amsterdam. He is also a cousin to Titus, through Titus's mother, and Titus's pretty new wife is Gerrit van Uylenburgh's cousin, too. All so cozy, so very *gezellig*. The old tie to the van

Uylenburghs that had been cut when Vader couldn't keep his hands off his maid—my mother—has been knotted again.

I follow Vader into Magdalena's house, ducking under the golden fish-shaped sign that swings above the door. Everyone blinks as we tumble from the dark into the great hall. Mirrors cover every wall, making the light from the bristling chandeliers painful to the eyes. Like everyone else, I clap blindly as Titus and Magdalena take their places on their wedding thrones canopied with a thick red-and-gold Turkey carpet. When I can see, I study Magdalena's pale hazel cat's eyes, her silky silver-blond hair, those high, wide cheekbones, that pointed little chin. I will never be that beautiful.

I hate her.

The viol and pipes quicken their tune. The jingle of gold deafens as the guests begin to clap. Though Vader has no gold chains to rattle, his grin grows wild. He puts his arm around the waist of the young woman next to him and leans to whisper in her ear. Oh, no, there he goes—fires burn in old houses. Please let him not embarrass Titus and me, not here, not now.

Since Magdalena's vader is dead, her cousin Gerrit comes forth with the double wedding goblet. The music builds to a screeching frenzy as bride and groom lean forward in their thrones to drink wine from great twin cups that swivel up from a connecting joint of silver. Titus gulps while Magdalena sips slowly, under protest, though both must drink every drop if they are to have good luck in their life together.

I feel someone watching me in the crowd of perfumed

well-wishers. Someone must have figured out I am Titus's ill-starred half sister. Cringing, I look toward the source and find a boy just older than I, watching me with his mouth slightly open. He looks away fast, not wanting to make a connection with the likes of me, so I stare back, daring him to look me in the eye. But as I study him in cold defiance, I notice his clear blue eyes. They are the very color of the irises that grow at the river's edge. And his spun-gold hair—see how sweetly the curls catch on the linen of his collar. His light brown lashes are as long as a girl's, though he is most definitely not a girl, not with those shoulders, not with those hands, and his upper lip is slightly fuller than the lower—

What am I doing, staring down such a boy like this? But before I can look away, he returns my gaze.

He smiles.

Heat comes so fast to my cheeks that I nearly drop from light-headedness, though I have the quickness of mind to pretend that I am merely looking at someone behind him—an old woman, it just so happens, whose chins are laid like a pale pudding upon the platter of her wagon-wheel ruff. Still smiling, he raises a brow then turns to follow my intent gaze. The old woman glares at him with an intensity that would singe the feathers off a goose. He frowns at the floor.

I am grinning when my sights catch on something on the wall behind Titus and Magdalena, still tipping back their wine cups: life-size portraits of the newlyweds. I didn't know Titus had asked Vader to paint their picture.

Then I see how smoothly the couple is painted, how there are no visible brushstrokes. Someone else has painted the wedding portrait of the great Rembrandt's son.

I move to grab Vader before he sees.

Too late.

"Van der Helst!" Vader's throaty voice cuts a swath through the squeal of the pipes as he elbows his way past gentlemen in their best black cassocks and ladies in their glossiest silks. His own dull doublet, layered over even older doublets for warmth, is stretched so tightly across his rounded shoulders that the seams pull. Why had I not thought to inspect his dress before we came? "Old Bartol van der Helst!" he exclaims. "His name is writ all over them!"

Magdalena pulls away sharply from her cup. The last of her wine spills out—three bloodred drops—and soaks into Titus's white collar. She presses her fingers on the spots as if to make them disappear, then bursts into tears. Magdalena's mother rushes to Magdalena; the bride throws herself into her mother's arms. The bagpipe wheezes to a stop.

Oblivious to it all, Vader arrives at the painting, folds his arms over his barrel chest, and cranes forward to better judge the portrait of Titus. There are yellow paint spots on the back of his doublet. "A fair likeness," he growls to himself. "A good one, most would think."

Five ladies in black gowns glossy as a rook's wing gather around Magdalena and her mother, patting the injured parties' backs. Guests lean together and whisper as Titus pulls on his collar to see what damage has been done. I slip a sickened glance at the handsome blond boy. He is staring at Vader with the rest of them.

Gerrit van Uylenburgh, more hat than man, steps in front of Vader. "Now look here, Rembrandt, the girl wanted their portraits done, and she wanted the most modern painter, that's all. Must you spoil her happiness on her wedding day?"

Golden chains clank as people shift uncomfortably; someone clears his throat. A sharp note rips from the viol as the fiddler drops his bow. Now Vader sees Magdalena clutching Titus's hand. He notes the glares shooting from the other guests. The crease that separates his brows deepens.

"I am sorry. I did not realize."

He snatches off his cap and bows, first kissing Magdalena's hand, then Titus's, then kisses them both on the cheeks, Magdalena as stiff in his hands as an ivory doll. "Best wishes to you, my children. May your marriage be a long and happy one. Good night."

"Don't go, Papa," says Titus.

Vader looks at Magdalena, and then at the angry relatives surrounding her. "Goodnight, my son." He starts toward the door, his bandy legs carrying his stocky body in an old man's shuffle. The guests shrink away from his path as if he has the tokens of the plague upon him.

The viol player taps out three beats and the pipes begin to wheeze.

"Papa!" Titus calls, then wildly scans the crowd. When he

finds me, the desperation in his face makes me want to cry. *Help,* he mouths.

Vader opens the door. A wind rushes inside, lifting heavy skirts and capes and rattling the mirrors on the wall. I'll not stop him.

Vader turns. When he meets Titus's gaze, Titus gives him such a raw look of love that it splits my heart.

"Goodnight, Vader."

One side of Vader's mouth crooks into a pained curve. "Goodnight, son."

He plunges into the night.

Magdalena's mother smoothes her daughter's hair. From under his large hat, Gerrit van Uylenburgh pours wine for two men wearing thick chains, while a man in a fur robe steps up and shakes Titus's hand. Titus tears his gaze from the door.

The old woman with the pudding chins and ruff turns and narrows her watery eyes at me. A young man catches her staring, sees me, then slaps the buck next to him with the red gloves he's holding. They smirk together. The handsome boy with the yellow curls takes it all in, frowning at me like he's trying to figure something out. I don't wait for him or anyone else to mock me. I slip through the crowd, my head pounding with shame.

Outside, the cold, fishy air bites my hot skin as I run down the brick sidewalk after Vader. I want to sink the boats rocking smugly on the Singel. Kick the rats scurrying in front of me. One night! Just one night! Why cannot Vader behave like everyone else just one night?

We tramp on through the dark streets, my anger not abating as we cross bridges and empty market squares, take turns down unfamiliar shadowy passages. I must keep Vader in view or lose my way, though the sight of his rounded back only fans my righteous fire. Narrower and narrower the streets become, until at last I recognize the neighborhood. A baby cries behind shuttered windows as we pass. Dogs bark. A woman shrieks from inside a dimly lit corner tavern. When the clouds scud from the moon to reveal triangular gabled rooftops crowded together like the broken teeth of a comb, I know we are almost home.

Inside the house, Vader lights a candle. He should not waste it. We can find our beds without it, enough milky moonlight is filtering through the windows.

Vader starts upstairs, though his bed is in the back room. Go to sleep, old candle waster. I head toward the kitchen, then remember with a jolt that I can now have Titus's bed—no longer do I have to sleep on my pallet by the fire. I am not cheered by this as much as I thought I would be.

In the front room, I take off my good skirt and bodice, push back the curtain, and slide in my shift under the featherbags on the four-poster bed. They smell like Titus—salty and sweetly musty, with a touch of spicy smoke. His joshing laugh comes to my ears. I see his angel face.

I turn over, unable to get comfortable. Who is going to

watch over me now that Titus is gone? Who is going to care two figs whether I come or whether I go?

The face of the handsome boy at the wedding floats into my mind. I sigh with happiness as I recall his smile when he saw me pretending to gaze at the old lady. He smiled at me, *me,* Cornelia, as if we had our own joke. I touch my face, with its cheekbones so like Moeder's, its silly little nose. Could he actually think me pretty?

And then I see him watching Vader, after Vader acted like a fool and made Magdalena spill her wine.

Overhead, the floorboards creak. The old man is still wasting candles. Someone should make good use of the light, and since I cannot sleep, I can do some mending. I haven't got a pair of stockings through which my big toe does not poke, and Vader is hardly going to pick up needle and thread.

Upstairs, a filmy shawl of moonlight rests on Vader's bent back, illuminating the yellow paint spots on his doublet as he stands before the painting of the van Roops, a candle flickering near the canvas. Tijger squats at his feet. Vader makes no sign that he sees me before he steps to the painting with his tiniest brush, the one made of ten sable hairs—the likes of which I would sneak from his palette when I was little, to rub across my cheek.

"Lord, grant me peace!" Vader growls, ordering his dear friend God Almighty as if He were a sulky servant. "Grant me peace!"

In spite of my anger, the movement of Vader's brush puts

me in a spell. I don't know how much time passes as Vader dots pinpoints of white around the baby's eyes, softening them, softening them. At last, in the guttering light of the candle, something is happening. My mending slips from my hand as I lean forward, holding my breath. I can see it—the love flowing from the baby's eyes. It is so calm, so pure, it fills me with rest.

With a start, I recognize the eyes.

They are Titus's.

Chapter 4

Two Moors.

1661. Canvas.

The snow comes down, muffling the cheerful tune of the carillon bells of the Westerkerk as I run home from school. The snow catches on the holly bushes, putting soft caps on the hard green leaves, but I only want Moeder. A girl in my class, Jannetje Zilver, has yelled at me for using her handkerchief, but I didn't know it was hers.

I fly across the bridge and up our steps. Moeder is not in the front room. She is not in the kitchen, nor cleaning, nor in the back sleeping. I take the stairs up two at a time.

Moeder is not in Vader's studio either. But Vader is there, behind his canvas. I shrink back when I see the two men bunched together before him like doves on a windowsill. Tijger winds between their feet as if claiming them for himself.

Vader looks over his shoulder. "Cornelia. Say hello to the gentlemen. Cornelia is six this year."

Vader is not mad at me for coming upstairs?

I know I should run before he shouts, but such a pair of men I have never seen. Vader has painted many different things in his studio, the strangest of which was a whole skinned ox, fresh from the butcher, but this pair, these men—their skin is the color of the chocolate Jannetje Zilver brings in her basket for her de noen. They are beautiful.

The taller man hides behind the littler one, his chin hooked on the little man's shoulder. His eyes are open but they don't seem to work. They are as blank as the floorboards, as if a thousand Jannetje Zilvers have shouted at him and he cannot take it anymore.

But the shorter dark man stands up straight. He is dressed in a king's gold clothes and like a king, holds his head high and has his hand on his hip. What I like best are his eyes, gray and shiny like the inside of an oyster, but brighter, like a candle burns from within him. When he turns them to me, they are so kind I burst into tears.

Moeder trudges up the stairs behind me. "Neeltje, when did you come—Why, you are crying! Come here, my pretty puss." She gathers me to her and takes me down to the kitchen.

She is giving me a dipper of water when Vader comes in. "I need some ale for the gentlemen," he says. He sees me. "What's the matter with her?"

"Can you not see? Your 'gentlemen' have scared her."

"Scared her? She is six, too old to be scared by such things." He leans toward me, bringing his gray bristly eyebrows close. "Cornelia, are you scared?"

I cry louder. I cannot stop. I wouldn't have used Jannetje's handkerchief if I had known it was hers.

"Why must you paint such terrible men?" Moeder says. "The Trip

brothers have decided to let you paint the portraits of their parents and you put them off to paint these, these—"

"—these men I must paint!"

She takes a short, angry breath. "But Rembrandt, you were so glad when the Trip brothers finally came to you. It was your chance to show up van der Helst and the lot. Why must you be so willful when we need the money?"

"I am not being willful, Hendrickje. I know this will sound strange—it does even to me—but I think God is speaking through my hands. Did you see the light I have captured in the little man's eyes?" He looks at his paint-speckled hands in wonder. "I don't know how I did that."

I had seen the light in the man's eyes in Vader's painting. Tears come down as I hold out the empty water dipper.

Moeder takes it, then puts her arm around me. "You are upsetting everyone," she tells Vader.

He looks at Moeder. "Are you sorry you chose me? Or do you wish you had chosen the man who owns men rather than paints them?"

"What has that to do with anything? And besides, Nicolaes owns the ships that carry them, not the men."

"What is the difference, Hendrickje? Whether he owns them or ships them, he's still got a hand in their misery, and no amount of money is going to wash that hand clean."

She presses me to her bodice. It smells of dried sweat. "Just give your people their ale."

After Vader is gone, I start to tell her about Jannetje.

"Is that what you are crying about? A handkerchief?" She puts her hand to my cheek. "It is snowing out. Go play." She gives me two pats.

But when I go outside, the sun is shining on the bare trees along the banks of the black canal. The snow is gone. I am too late.

A man comes over the bridge. When he tips his hat at me, I see his mustache in the shade of his brim. It is as gold as the coins Moeder keeps hidden in a leather pouch in the back of her cupboard.

He taps his finger to his lip. "Shhhh."

"Shhhh," I say back, tapping my mouth.

It is our game.

I've seen this man before. He is tall and has curly gold hair down to his shoulders and gold hairs over his mouth.

He smiles, then goes on his way without another sound, as he always does. He is just a nice neighbor man. I want to ask Moeder who he is, but she is never outside when he passes.

I crouch at the edge of the canal and throw in a stone.

Chapter 5

Vader roars from his studio, "TITUS!"

I turn the page of my book and stir the cabbage, Tijger rubbing against my stool, as the wind rattles the rose vine outside the kitchen window. It is the third of March, three days since the wedding, and the old man cannot get it in his head that Titus is gone.

"TITUS! COME QUICKLY!"

Why should I tend to a stubborn old man who cared so little about me that he tossed a secondhand name my way when I was born? Cornelia was the name of his first two daughters by Titus's mother. Both died young, within days of their birth. Though it is customary to name girls after their grandmother, after the second death, one would begin to think about the luck that name carries. I do.

The front door opens. I hide my book under my apron.

With Titus gone, it could only be Neel. Sure enough, he leans his head into the kitchen.

A grimace of apology flashes across Neel Suythof's long face before it resumes its somber appearance. "Hello, Cornelia."

It would not put him in the grave to smile once in a while. If he did, the faded marks left on his neck by a childhood case of the pox would be almost unnoticeable. He might never be as handsome as the golden-haired boy at the wedding, but then, who is?

"Hello, Neel."

Tijger strolls over to him to beg a petting. Neel bends down to stroke him. "Have you heard from Titus yet?"

"No, and I do not expect to."

He regards me soberly over Tijger's loud rumbling. "How was the wedding?"

I shrug. Maybe it hasn't gotten around yet how Vader brought bad luck upon his own son's marriage.

There is a look of sympathy in Neel's plain brown eyes. It makes me uncomfortable.

"You miss Titus," he says.

"Why would I miss him? He is a grown man. He is supposed to be wed. And Magdalena was quite the catch."

A roar comes again from upstairs: "TITUS!"

I roll my gaze to the ceiling. "Apparently, someone *does* miss Titus." I untie my apron and slip out from under it with my book still hidden, leaving both on my stool. I ladle soup into a cracked bowl. "Here, take him his dinner, would you?"

"TITUS, LAD!"

Neel looks up, too, as if he could see Vader through the ceiling. "Does he not know Titus is not here?"

"The question is, has he ever figured out that I *am* here?"

Neel gazes at me.

I should have never spoken out. Neel Suythof needs not know what goes on in our family. Let him be starry-eyed over his hero. He might be the last person in Amsterdam to admire Rembrandt van Rijn.

"Just take him his dinner, please."

Neel's hand brushes mine as he takes the tray from me. I rub my hand as he leaves the kitchen, Tijger following after him. Of course Neel's touch is warm—he is alive, isn't he?

A few moments later, Neel plods back down the stairs to the kitchen. "Your vader said the soup needs salt."

There was a reason I had skimped on salt—to put a name on it, poverty—but I cannot tell Neel this. If he realized how low Vader's star has sunk, he might quit his lessons, then where would we be? Neel's measly stuivers mean bread on the table.

I hand him the saltcellar. "Be careful not to spill it," I say, as if I were the adult and he the child.

"As you wish, madam."

I look at him and see a hint of a smile in his eyes. His lightheartedness surprises me. "Vader's waiting for his salt," I say gruffly.

The cheer goes out of his face. "Of course."

I frown at my apron on the stool as he goes back upstairs. Why must I always do the wrong thing, like pretending to look at an old lady when the handsome boy caught me staring at him at the wedding? Neel the Serious almost smiled and I struck him down.

I hear the front door open. Titus bounds into the kitchen.

"Worry Bird!" He grabs me and swings me around until I knock over my stool. My book flaps to the floor. He beats me to picking it up. "*The Marriage Trap*?"

"You should read it," I say, blushing fiercely. "To see what a predicament you are in. What are you doing here, anyway?"

"Bird, you are harsh. And why would I not be here? This is my home."

"*Was* your home."

He puts on a mock-sad face. "I am not welcome here, and apparently, I am trapped in marriage. Whatever am I going to do?"

The crabbiness in which Neel has left me only deepens. I shall be as much of an ogre as Vader before too long. "Don't laugh. Soon Magdalena will insist on having all of her friends over for chocolate and you will be required to stay and entertain them."

"I like chocolate."

"And then she's going to spend all your money and make you turn to drink."

"Oh, good, then I shall come see you on my way to the tavern." He lunges forward to pinch me.

I dodge him handily. "I don't believe that. It has been ages since you've been back."

"Bird, it has been three days. I just was wed!"

"See? She owns you now. Just like the book says."

Neel returns to the kitchen. He stops upon seeing Titus.

"Neel, how are you? Paint anything good lately?" Titus raises a brow and smiles.

"I am learning," Neel says.

Titus lowers my book, smiling, and waits for more.

A spot of red creeps up each of Neel's cheeks. "Your vader asks for ale," he says to me. Neel is just five years younger than Titus, but he acts as if my brother bewilders him.

I pluck my book from Titus's hands, shove it under the clothes to be ironed that are piled on the table, then pour ale from the jug. I hold out the pewter mug to Neel.

"Let me know when you have a painting you would like me to sell," Titus calls after him as he walks away. "Just as charming as ever," he says with a grin.

"We cannot all be as charming as you," I reply, surprised by a jolt of sympathy for Neel.

"Oh, hush," Titus protests, but I see him glance at his own reflection in the window. "Neel's a good enough fellow. A bit serious, perhaps . . ."

I pick up an unironed collar from the table, pretend to fold it, then throw it down. "I cannot stand it around here. Vader is going crazy. He keeps calling for you, when he has to know you are gone."

Titus pulls back in surprise. "He does?"

"All the time."

"He never used to be confused," says Titus. "Tactless and absurd, yes, but not confused. Maybe I should call a physician."

"No!" I say. Doctors cost money. "Maybe it's not that bad."

"TITUS!" Vader yells from upstairs.

Titus looks at me. "Is that what he's been doing?"

His worried face alarms me. Maybe Vader is worse than I feared. Maybe the eccentricity that has always shamed us has tipped more deeply into madness than I had thought. "Neel must have told him you were here."

"TITUS!"

Titus races from the kitchen, then leaps up the stairs three at a time, with me trailing after him. He has Vader in a bear hug before I reach the studio.

"Papa!" Titus looks at Vader tenderly. "Did Neel tell you I was here?"

Neel, holding Vader's mug of ale, shakes his head no.

Vader's saggy cheeks, shadowed by white stubble from not shaving since Titus's wedding day, rise in a joyous grin. "A wonderful surprise!" He embraces Titus and thumps him on the back. "How are you, lad?" he cries in his throaty voice.

Titus pulls back. "Papa, I heard you call me. Do you not know I have left? I am married now."

"Of course I know," says Vader. "To Saskia's cousin. Lovely girl."

"Then why do you do it? Cornelia says you shout after me all day long."

Vader shrugs merrily, a paint-splotched St. Nicolaes. All he needs is presents for the little children. "It makes me feel better to pretend you are here."

Titus and I exchange a look. Perhaps he is just being a nuisance after all.

Titus sucks in his breath. "Papa, Cornelia will take care of you now."

"Cornelia?" Vader squints at me like a blind man.

"When you call for me knowing I am gone, it scares her," Titus says. "It scares me, too."

"You children scare too easy. Neel, where is my ale?"

Neel steps forward with the mug. He glances at me as Vader guzzles. I make my face as blank as possible. Neel need not know how worried I am about Vader.

"What I am saying, Papa," says Titus, "is that when you need something, call Cornelia."

"I will, I will." Vader takes another deep draw from his ale. "I never worry about Cornelia."

I won't let them see me wince. Am I not worth worrying about?

Vader points with his mug toward the painting of the family scene resting on the easel. "What do you think?" he asks Titus.

Titus leans forward to examine it.

"Not so close! The smell of paint will not agree with you."

Titus laughs. "Do not use that old line with me—I've got paint running through my blood. I won't look too closely at the brushstrokes, if that's what you want." He steps back.

"Excellent likenesses, Papa. It's the van Roops from across the courtyard, isn't it?"

"Very good." Vader's smile becomes sly. "Do you notice anything else?"

Neel flashes me a conspiratory glance but I won't acknowledge him. If he recognizes Titus's eyes in the picture, it is because he's had time to study it.

"You use more gold pigment in your reds these days," says Titus.

Vader folds his arms over his chest, his grin deepening. "And?"

Titus looks again at the canvas, then takes on a scolding tone. "Papa, you're loading your paint with charcoal powder. Those dabs on the baby's skirts are so thick they stand out from the canvas. You could use them as handles to pick up the painting." Then he brightens. "Have you got a buyer?"

As miserable as Vader makes me, I cannot bear the look of hopeful anticipation on his face. "The eyes," I whisper to Titus.

He doesn't hear me. "I don't know what you want me to say, Papa," he says. "It looks good. The painting is very good."

Vader holds onto the tail end of his smile. "Thank you, son."

"Keep up the good work." Titus claps him on the back. "Someone is sure to buy it. And I've got new contacts now, through Magdalena. All those years you trained me for the art market are finally going to pay off."

"Good, son. Good." Vader's gaze is on the painting.

"Papa?"

Vader doesn't answer; he's looking at the picture. There is pity in Neel's eyes as he watches him. Can Neel see what Vader's own son cannot?

"Papa?" says Titus. "I brought two rounds of Edam cheese. There is a bottle of port for you, too. Magdalena won't miss it—we have got a whole cellarful."

"What?"

"*Cheese*, Papa, I brought you some."

"Oh." Vader turns away from the easel, his jaw set as if he has made a decision. "Thank you, son." He smiles, but the light has left his pale green eyes.

Neel looks at me, but I will not look back. He should not judge Titus. Titus has been through more than he ever will. Titus and I together.

"Oh, and Bird," Titus says, "before I go, I have been meaning to tell you—you had better be more careful about keeping the street clean in front of the house. Cases of the pestilence have been reported in town, and there is a new ordinance that all residents must sweep their streets each day." He sees my expression. "Don't worry, they think the sickness can be kept from spreading this way."

"It is not in our hands, regardless," Vader mutters, more to his painting than to us.

Chapter 6

The Sampling Officials.

1662. Canvas.

Shouts, coming from outside, wake me on my pallet. I hear scraping sounds.

I throw back my feather bag, hop across the cold tiles, then wipe the frost from the window with my shift front. Outside on the canal, two boys skate by. A mother pulls a sled with a bundled-up baby on it.

"It froze!" I whisper.

I pull on my clothes and run through the house, my shawl flapping like a seabird. "It froze! It froze! Titus! The canal has frozen!"

In the hall I nearly trip over Tijger, who runs away, his tail arched like a monkey's. Moeder is peeling an onion in the kitchen.

"Moeder, the canal is frozen!"

"Neeltje, shhh!"

I peer out the kitchen window. "Why didn't you wake me?"

Out on the canal, our neighbors, Mijnheer *and* Mevrouw *Bicker, he tall and thin, she as small, round, and neat as a jam pot, skate by slowly, holding hands with their son and three little daughters, who are chopping along on their own little skates. Behind them, an old couple glides along in step, their windburned faces serious. They frown at the pack of boys yelling and racing toward them, all flapping scarves and chapped cheeks.*

"Everyone's skating! Let's go!"

"I can't, puss. I must have a nice soup available for de noen—Vader is expecting an important visitor. The sampling officials of the Draper's Guild are considering your vader for their group portrait."

Outside the window, one of the Bicker girls falls on the ice, her legs straight out in front of her. She starts to cry until little Mevrouw Bicker plucks her up from under her arms and spins her in a circle until she laughs.

"Why can't we have fun like everyone else?"

"Shh, puss, we'll go out later. You'll just have to wait."

"Where is Titus?"

"At his aunt's."

"Not again!" All I hear when Titus comes back from the van Loos' is about his pretty cousin Magdalena. I stomp to the stairs to Vader's studio and hang on the banisters. Why must I always wait? I hang upside down with my hair brushing the floor until my head gets tingly, then swing myself up the stairs.

I crouch down in the doorway at the top. Vader is standing in his studio, with palette and brushes in hand. I am not allowed to be here. I should run back downstairs, but I like the way he looks. I like his square back, his thick arms holding the painting things, the gray curls coming out the bottom of his cap. I want to sit by him and smell his spicy skin.

"Cornelia," Vader growls, "what are you doing?"

Someone calls, "Hallo, little miss."

I peek past Vader's legs. A man in a golden robe sits at a table to the side of Vader's easel. He's holding a sword as thick as his hairy hand. His face is mostly covered in beard, but where one of his eyes should be is an empty flap of skin.

I scramble backward like a crab, then fall on my back.

He scratches his beard, brown and bristly as the rat-catcher's dog, with the tip of his sword. "She's afraid of the weapon. Don't worry, miss, there's no edge to it. It couldn't slice a round of cheese." He whacks his own arm to prove it. No blood.

"Cornelia," Vader says, "say hello to Mijnheer Gootman."

"Make that Claudius Civilis," the man says stoutly, lifting his sword. "Ain't I a handsome king?"

I can't look at him. What if the flap comes open?

"Sorry, mijnheer," Vader says, "she's a skittish one."

"Let her be," Mijnheer Gootman says. "I had my own little schaapje, *little Trientje. She was a shy one, too. Taken by the plague, she was, just last summer."*

"Sorry to hear that," Vader says. "I lost my first child that way."

"It was a hard time for the wife and me." Mijnheer Gootman sighs loudly, then a smile lifts his beard. "I saw you watching your vader paint, miss. Are you going to be a painter like your old pa?"

I sit up. Paint stinks but I don't mind. I would like to paint like Vader, to make things come alive in pictures.

"That's hardly likely," Vader mutters.

"Because she's a girl?" says Mijnheer Gootman. "Do not underestimate a woman, my friend. How many widows have you seen take over their dead husband's shop and build up the business tenfold?"

"It's not that Cornelia is a girl," Vader mutters.

Footsteps tap briskly up the stairs. A man in a glossy black cape arrives at the studio door, then steps over me. With a smell of flowers, he puts out a yellow-gloved hand. "Rembrandt."

Vader shifts his brushes to his other hand to shake. "Mijnheer van Neve." He nods to the one-eyed man. "This is Jan Gootman. He is a cobbler from down the street."

Mijnheer Gootman leans on the table and sticks out his own hairy hand to Mijnheer van Neve as Vader goes back to painting. The fancy man curls his lip at Mijnheer Gootman's paw, like he has sniffed a rotten onion.

"Sorry, Rembrandt," Mijnheer van Neve says as Vader dabs at the canvas. "I did not know you were working. Your . . . wife . . . sent me up." Behind Vader's back, he narrows his eyes at me and smiles as if he has heard something naughty. "I shall come back later."

"No need." Vader loads his brush with black. "If you've come to discuss the terms for your group portrait of the sampling officials, I can do so now as I paint. I've got to keep working on this piece for the new Town Hall. I suppose you heard I won that commission—the biggest picture in the building. Quite a project."

But the fancy man is already leaving. "I shall come back."

Vader stops painting. "Mijnheer van Neve—"

"I shall be back."

Mijnheer Gootman is still frowning at his unshaken hand as the fancy man goes down the stairs. Vader turns back to him and sighs. "Now where were we, my friend?"

I stand up, put my arms on top my head, and twist so my skirt swirls this way and that to get Mijnheer Gootman to notice me. Please talk some more about girls like me painting. Because I want to paint. More than anything.

But Mijnheer Gootman only uses the tip of his blunt sword to push up the crown sliding down his forehead. "How much longer do you think it will be, Mijnheer van Rijn? If I'm gone too long from the shop, there will be hell to pay with the wife."

Chapter 7

It has been two weeks since Titus left me for Magdalena and the House of the Gilded Scales. It is an unusually fine day for mid-March. A few furry scraps of clouds creep across a sky as blue as the expensive chunks of lapis lazuli Vader grinds for his paint. A breeze damp with the sea plucks at my skirt as I stand at the edge of the canal with Tijger, who has followed me outside, his majestic strut lending my lowly errand a more regal air. Save for the soft plopping sound of the boats tied in the canal, and the screech of the gulls, it seems oddly quiet, until the death bells of the Westerkerk break the silence. A shiver of fear runs through me, then I shake it off. It is probably not the plague. A person rich enough to buy the bell ringer's services has died of something else. Let us all weep buckets.

Vader's shout sails out the upper window. "CORNELIA!"

Not again.

In the canal, a brown mother duck and her five fist-sized yellow ducklings slice through my reflection in the murky water. I pour the contents of the slop jar into the canal, well away from them. Maybe if I ignore Vader he will forget about me.

"Cornelia! Do not waste time!"

I groan when I see a passenger boat approaching, pulled from the other side of the canal by a boy on a bony black horse. I hurry into the house before the passengers, seated around the edges of the boat, can hear him. Now that Vader has been told to call for me, he does it day and night. Why did we tell him not to shout for Titus?

I find Vader in the back room, sitting on the steps to his bed-cupboard. He is putting on his shoes.

"What is it?" I ask.

"I need to be shaved. I am going out."

"So go to a surgeon, like everyone else," I say, though I know we can't afford it.

He points to a bowl on the floor. There is a razor, strap, and sponge in it.

"You want me to shave you? I don't know how to shave!"

"There's a piece of soap in the bowl—suds it up, slap it on." He pats his face to demonstrate. "There's nothing to it. Titus used to do it for me."

I grimace at the grizzled tufts sprouting from his leathery cheeks and chin. He has not shaved since Titus's marriage. For that matter, he has not gone out but has shut himself up in his studio, painting a portrait of himself. The man has more portraits of himself than the king of Spain.

"I can't shave you." I cringe at the thought of him wandering around in public, shaved or not. "Where are you going?"

He chuckles as if to let me in on a lark. "To pay Gerrit van Uylenburgh a visit. We will see if the young shoot's taste for art has improved or if he remains as thickheaded as his vader. Old Hendrick was a dull old ox if I ever saw one. A stuiver-pincher, too."

I wince. "Mijnheer van Uylenburgh won't talk to you! Don't you remember what you did at the wedding?"

"What?"

"The wine!"

"What?"

"You made Magdalena spill it. You cursed their marriage!"

"Oh, that. It was an accident. Besides, who believes in that superstitious nonsense?"

"Magdalena's mother, for one. Those were not tears of joy she was crying when Magdalena was wiping Titus's collar."

Vader scowls at me for reminding him. "Well, this is business. If there is a guilder to be made, van Uylenburgh will be for it."

"But he has sold few of your paintings since . . ." I cross my arms. It was not my fault Vader took up with his maid. I did not ask to be born.

"I have not given him anything to sell."

That cannot be true, but there is no arguing with the man.

"Maybe you ought to let Titus talk to him first, now that their ties are stronger."

"No need. I will let my painting do the talking."

"Which painting?"

"The family group." He finishes with his shoes, then puts his hands on his knees, elbows out. "I no longer need it."

I want to shout a protest. I love that picture—the look in the baby's eyes is all I have of Titus now that he's Magdalena's, but I don't say a word. We need the money too badly. "I think we should wait for Titus."

"Nonsense."

"That picture is still on stretchers. How are you to carry it? It's huge."

"In the handcart. Get the razor."

I don't like the looks of the razor's edge, gleaming against the dull pottery of the bowl. "Why do you not shave yourself?"

Vader holds up his hands. "Palsy."

It is true, each finger trembles independently, as if inhabited by separate creatures. He must be pretending.

"Stop it."

He looks helplessly at his hands. "I can't."

"Then how do you paint?"

"God stills them."

The hair rises on my arms.

I must stay calm and not provoke him further. I steady my voice. "I cannot shave you, Vader. I will cut you."

"I won't let you."

I continue to protest, but he wears me down as usual and finally gets his way. When I am done, I have nicked him only five or six times around the chin—a most satisfactory job, considering the loose skin I have to navigate on his jowls. Soon we have breakfasted on ale and bread, and Vader has wrapped the painting in a linen drape and is buttoning up the paint- and ale-stained doublet that might have fit him when he was a young blade but from which he bursts like a sausage from its casing now.

"Come with me," he says.

It occurs to me that the child who resulted from the affair that caused the rift between him and the van Uylenburgh family thirteen years ago might not aid in the sale of this painting. "No."

"I need you to steady it in the cart."

My stare is not sympathetic. But it is wasted on the back of his head as he fetches the handcart from the courtyard, cursing as he untangles it from the thorn-covered canes of the rose vine. He maneuvers it inside and in front of the painting, making muddy tracks on the tiles that I will have to clean.

"There is big money in this," he says, "but if you won't go, I won't go either."

"Why?" I say, completely puzzled.

"Just . . ." He lifts the wrapped picture and, grunting, puts it in the cart. ". . . because."

The man's nerve is exceeded only by his madness. But I have finished *The Marriage Trap* and haven't been able to exchange it for another book at the bookseller's shop and so have nothing to do but while away the time at home with the kitchen rats. Besides, the painting might get damaged if Vader moves it by himself. Soon we are on our way to the bridge past the New Maze Park, Vader pulling the cart, me trying to steady the picture as the wooden wheels rattle over the cobblestones that pave the center of our street.

Tijger follows us over the humpbacked brick bridge and past the hedges of the park, behind which the peacocks squawk as if they are being wrung for someone's supper. "Go home," I tell him, "before you get lost."

He looks up at me, his tail swaying in languid unconcern.

Vader stops the cart to stamp his foot. "Shoo!"

Tijger sits down.

"Oh, well," Vader says to Tijger. "You've figured out how to get us to wait on you hand and foot all these years, you can figure out how to get yourself home now."

I fret over Tijger's safety as he trails us again as we resume our clumsy journey with the cart. Tijger amuses Vader. Vader has sketched him many times—bathing, sleeping, scratching behind his ear. Tijger appears several times in the large-and-growing gallery of unsold paintings on the wall in the front room of our house.

I appear not once.

We go two streets to where there is a small poultry market surrounding the crossroads. I keep my head down as we cross diagonally to the far corner, passing ladies with their maids carrying baskets on their arms and girls selling eggs cradled in their aprons. A black-painted carriage rattles by, its springs squeaking. Two men walk past, then turn to look at Vader, who is a sight enough, pulling a child's cart, though his idiot's appearance is only compounded by his wisps of white hair waving about in the damp March wind. Rembrandt van Rijn might be the only man in Amsterdam not wearing a wide-brimmed black hat. I tug my own linen cap down by its strings, glad I have worn my hair loose so it can hang over my face. So keen am I not to be recognized, that it is not until we turn the corner onto the Lauriergracht that I realize Tijger is missing.

"Tijger!"

"Don't worry about him," said Vader. "He'll go home."

"What if he gets crushed by a carriage or chased by dogs? What if—" I stop, not wanting to give credence to a terrible thought: in times of plague, cats and dogs on the streets are rounded up and destroyed, for some believe they are carriers. During the last terrible pestilence, I'd had to keep him in the house . . . before we were locked in ourselves.

Vader studies my face. "You worry too much."

"You don't worry enough."

He raises his gray brows at me.

"You don't," I say, standing my ground.

"What good does worrying do?" he says. "Has it ever changed the course of anything?"

"Let's just go home," I say miserably.

He shakes his head. "We're here now."

He points to the house just ahead. The building is one of a row of houses four stories high and four windows wide—palaces, compared to ours. Van Uylenburgh's house might be just a canal away in distance, but it is a world away in style. Dealers of art must fare better than the artists themselves—at least in Vader's case.

I glance at my brown wool dress and thin apron, then at Vader in his paint-spotted, ale-stained, belly-gapping doublet, with his set of bloody chicken tracks on his jowls. We make a ridiculous picture—two beggars with a rag cart—as we approach the porch steps.

"Let me go over and wait on the bridge."

Vader grabs my arm as I start to cross back across the street. "Nonsense. I want you to see the young pinch-stuiver's face when he beholds this piece. He has had a steady diet of ordinariness—it's about time he gets a little dessert." He lets go of my arm to knock on the tall red-varnished door. A young woman in a winged white cap, blue gown, and starched collar and apron answers before I can run.

"Is your master here?" Vader asks.

I study the woman. How did Vader know she was a maid? She is dressed far better than I.

She looks him up and down, disapproval writ all over the pink cheeks of her fresh-from-the-countryside face. "Who should I say is calling?"

"Rembrandt," says Vader.

She peers at him with interest, then bangs the door shut.

I hear the voices of men inside. What if Gerrit van Uylenburgh doesn't want the picture and Vader gets nasty? I think of the time a merchant from the East India Company came to see about having his portrait made. When he saw the pictures on our wall, he said that he was looking for something more modern and smooth and less lumpy. Vader threw a bowl, missing the merchant by a hairsbreadth. "I shall give you lumpy!" he cried.

Fear mushrooms inside me. "Vader, remember, you can catch more flies with honey than vinegar!"

Vader looks at me as if I am the cracked one.

"Use your charm," I say helplessly.

Vader laughs. "Charm?" He shifts on his feet. "What is taking him?"

A boy not much older than me opens the door. He is slender yet powerfully built and has curls of spun gold, and now, upon seeing my vader on the stoop, there is surprise in the eyes as blue as the irises that grow at the river's edge.

Dear Lord, the boy from the wedding. What is he doing here?

"Who are you?" Vader says.

"Carel Bruyningh. Mijnheer van Uylenburgh's agent." He tilts his head and looks at me.

He will never remember me. In my plain clothes and with my plain hair, I am completely unmemorable, or, worse, if he does remember me, it will be as the daughter of the fallen painter Rembrandt.

"Since when," Vader says, "does young Gerrit send a pup to represent him?"

Dear Lord, let me run!

The handsome Carel straightens. "I know about art, sir. I am working on my masterpiece—I expect to be admitted to the guild quite soon though I am only sixteen." He raises his chin. "I study with Ferdinand Bol."

"Then you have a lot of unlearning to do," says Vader. Before Carel can react, Vader says, "A Bruyningh. Any relation to Nicolaes?"

Oh, dear Lord, just let me go!

"He is my uncle, mijnheer. I am familiar with the portrait you painted of him—a powerful piece of work. It is in his house. You did it several years ago."

"Fifteen years to be exact." Vader stares at him in a very rude way. "And how is our dear Nicolaes these days?"

"Quite well, mijnheer." The boy glances at me. I study van Uylenburgh's house as if I had great interest in architecture, though pretending to look at something has not worked well for me in the past.

"Did he ever find himself a wife?" Vader asks.

I know now that I shall die from embarrassment. Does Vader know no bounds?

But Carel just laughs. "Uncle Nicolaes? Not yet." He holds out his hand for Vader to shake. His fingers look thick and strong, and though there is green paint under his nails, his hands are smooth. I slink my own rough hands behind my back.

"I am honored to meet you," he tells Vader. "You are a legend."

"I'm not dead yet," Vader growls.

"No, mijnheer! I did not mean—" The boy breaks off, blushing.

Vader peers over Carel's shoulder. "Where is Gerrit?"

"I am afraid he is busy, mijnheer. But I am authorized to act for him." He looks at me. "I saw you at the wedding. Are you Mijnheer van Rijn's daughter?"

If I could shrivel into dust and be blown to the winds, I should welcome it, but there is no such escape for me. I smile weakly, then touch Vader's arm. "We should go."

Vader shakes me off. "I shall speak only to Gerrit," he tells Carel.

"So sorry, mijnheer," Carel says, his pale brows knitted in what I would think was true regret had I not known what a ridiculous figure Vader cuts. "He is not available."

"Well, I am not available to show my work to children."

"I am sorry, mijnheer, truly." Carel's face is red. He glances at me. I pick at my apron as if a speck of lint has so completely captured my attention that I have not heard Vader insult him.

Vader rips the drape from the painting that sits cockeyed in the wagon. "What will your master say when he finds he has missed this?"

Carel's mouth eases open as he beholds the painting of the van Roop family. At last he says, "Nice."

"Nice?" says Vader.

"I know it is good—very good. Still, I cannot take it."

Vader's voice drips with sarcasm: *"You know it is 'good' and you 'cannot take it'?"*

"Mijnheer, if you please, look at those globs of paint. Even I know there is no market for rough stuff like that. Have you not seen Bol's work? Or Nicholas Maes's?"

"Dullheaded students of mine," Vader says. "You lost your chance." He hastily throws the linen over the painting, then storms away, dragging the cart behind him like a five-year-old with his play-cart. I follow like a whipped hound.

"I am sorry, mijnheer!" Carel calls after us. "Good-bye, Miss—Miss . . ."

I fight off the desire to give him one last look—I cannot, no, *I will not* take the risk of finding a smirk upon his handsome face.

As we retreat down the walkway, more crowded now with midmorning activity, there are no words sharp enough to rain upon my vader, none that will penetrate his thick skin and wound him as his actions have wounded me. It is enough that he shames me before our neighbors and Titus's relatives and anyone else we come into contact with, but to humiliate me in front of a handsome boy who actually remembered me—*me,* Cornelia—it is unbearable. I stalk behind him, my face down so as not to meet the eyes of the passersby, but by the time we reach the poultry market around the corner, I can no longer hold it in.

I wait until a young woman in a green cape and her servant,

an older woman, move beyond hearing. "We should not have gone," I scold.

Vader stops pulling the rattling cart and whirls around in the center of the busy crossroads. "What?"

I meet his irritable gaze, though it would be easier to hold my hand to coals. "We should not have gone." I hold my voice down for privacy, grateful for the hens screeching in the stalls around us. "You shame me."

"You're ashamed?" he says, raising his voice.

A woman hurries by, holding the hands of her two little sons. She flicks us a worried glance.

"Yes," I whisper. "Shhh!"

His voice grows louder. "You think I don't feel shame?"

This is why I don't speak up. "Vader—"

"I am sick with it! Sick! But I embrace it." He pounds his chest with his fist. "I take it to my heart like my bride."

Two women with market baskets on their arms and their mouths hanging open back toward the string of plucked ducks hanging behind them. Vader does not see them, or if he does, he does not care.

"My shame is a gift!" he shouts. "It is my cross and I thank my God for it. How can you ever feel mercy if you have never carried a cross?"

A poultryman, wiping his bloody knife on his apron, moves around the row of naked birds hanging from his stall to join the women.

"Chiaroscuro," Vader growls. "Do you know what that is?"

"Yes," I whisper quickly, "light against darkness—shhhh. Please, let us go."

"Light against darkness, the first principle of painting. What is light without darkness to set it off? Same goes for joy and pain. How are you to savor joy if you have never known pain?" Only then does he notice the crowd he has drawn. "What are you people staring at?"

A woman struts up like one of the hens she has come to buy. "Miss, are you unharmed?" she asks me.

"Of course she is," Vader snaps.

"I asked the girl," the woman says.

Shock ties my tongue. Let me sink onto these fowl-shat stones and die.

Housewives, poultrymen, and maidservants all stare as Vader snatches up the handle of his cart and stalks away with his rattling burden.

"Are you unharmed?" the woman asks me again.

I nod as Vader rounds the corner, my gaze following the hastily covered painting. Left to bash against the sides of the cart, it is taking a battering.

I almost laugh. I have been shamed to my very core and I am worrying about Vader's painting? It is only brushstrokes on canvas! What do I care?

"Thank you most kindly, mevrouw," I say as politely as one of the heroines in my books, then start after Vader, allowing enough distance to leave the question open to the crowd as to whether or not I actually know him.

"Crazy man," mutters the poultryman.

Something burns in my chest. No matter how often I call Vader crazy, it still wounds me when others do so.

Tijger is waiting on the stoop when I return. He protests loudly as I pick him up—he has not asked to be held—but I need him now. Only after we sit on the step for a while, his skinny tail thrashing my skirt, do I realize the death bells of the Westerkerk are tolling again. Damn them! *Now* they ring—lately three times a day it seems—when they would not ring for the sweetest, most gentle person in the world upon her burial. They stayed mute, hateful things, because Vader couldn't pay. He couldn't scrape together the guilders for the woman who stayed with him though shamed and rejected, who had hung on to his business when he could not, who had humored him through his moods, warmed his bed, raised his child. In life, he would never grant her dearest wish and marry her and legitimize his child—at least in death he could have bought her bells. But he didn't. Not Vader. My moeder went into the ground in silence.

Chapter 8

The Oath of Claudius Civilis.

Ca. 1661–1662.

Canvas, cut down to 196 × 309 cm.

"Here it is," Moeder says. "The new Town Hall."

She looks up, her hood falling back, as we stand among groups of men striding past in clean black doublets. Horses clop by, drawing wagons that creak under the weight of the barrels piled on top; peddlers shout about their wonderful apples! cheeses! rattraps! Skinny dogs sniff along the paving bricks, pushing around leaves that have blown from the trees along the canal. Moeder shades her eyes and clutches at something under her cape strings—the red-bead necklace she put on just before we left home. She wears it only when she goes out, and even then, she keeps it hidden—a terrible crime, in my opinion. It is the prettiest thing she owns. I don't know why she doesn't show it off.

I hold on to my own hood and tip my head back as far as it will go. The Town Hall is bigger than all of the buildings in the biggest square in town, and the biggest painting in it, the one we've come to see, is Vader's. My vader's.

Moeder and I look at each other and smile.

Inside the Town Hall, the sound of men talking and the tapping of their boots echoes off the high ceiling. I touch the smooth white walls. Though it is just October, they are as cold as a windowpane in winter.

Moeder nods like she owns the place. "It's marble, all of it—walls, floors."

Ahead is a huge picture on the wall. I run toward it, my clompen making a cracking noise on the shiny floor like wood being split, but see right away that the man in it has two eyes. It is not Mijnheer Gootman. There are more paintings, big ones like Vader's. I run from picture to picture, looking for Mijnheer Gootman in his crown. "Moeder, where is it?"

Moeder is turning like a hen on a spit. "Rembrandt said it was in the main hall, right as you walked in."

"Maybe this isn't the main hall."

"Yes, pretty puss," she says, twisting her necklace. "That's probably it."

She takes my hand and we walk this way and that, poking our heads inside doorways, where men in tall black hats stand talking. Most of the men don't see us, or at least they act like they don't, but some frown. A black-haired one with a pointed beard winks at Moeder, then laughs.

We go back to the big room. Moeder is drooping like a tulip in the frost, when her eyes light up.

"Mijnheer Bol!" She drags me toward a thick-bellied man with a plume in his hat. When he turns and sees us, one of his arched brows arches even higher in his heavy face.

"Mijnheer Bol!" Moeder is panting hard. "Thank God! I have been

looking for Rembrandt's painting and cannot find it. Can you please tell me where it is?"

His gaze goes up and down over Moeder.

Moeder blinks. "I'm sorry, I should have asked—where is your painting? Rembrandt told me you have a painting here, too."

The man turns away without a word, plume wafting, the tap of his heels echoing off the walls. Moeder doesn't move.

Moeder shakes me off her arm like I am dishwater. "All right, Cornelia! We are going. Please don't jump on me again."

She does not speak on the way home, even when the death bells of the Westerkerk bellow out and we must stop for a long procession of mourners in black robes. We are almost home when, just ahead, an oxcart stops in front of our house. It takes two big men to carry the rolled-up canvas to the stoop, their boots crunching the fallen leaves.

Vader answers the door.

Moeder stops. I look up. Her face has gone as white as the marble in the Town Hall.

The men are coming back down the steps of the stoop. They don't look at Moeder as she runs into the house.

Vader is unrolling the big canvas on the front-room floor. I see Mijnheer Gootman in his crown, his one good eye staring.

"I don't understand," Moeder says.

"What is there to understand?" Vader growls. "They didn't want it."

He goes to the kitchen and comes back with a knife.

Moeder screams. "Rembrandt, no!"

Vader drops to his knees on top of the picture. He holds out a corner, stabs in his knife, and rips.

I start to cry.

Moeder rushes over and tugs at the back of Vader's doublet. "Rembrandt, please! You can still sell it."

Vader shakes her off, tears off a strip of canvas, and tosses it aside. It flaps like a shot bird to the floor.

He is ready to stab again, when he sees me. "What is wrong with you?"

I swipe my face with my arm. Hurting the picture is like hurting me. I love it. Every thick stroke of it. Every stroke is a part of the story.

"Shut her up, Hendrickje."

"I can't."

"I said shut your brat up!"

"Rembrandt," Moeder sobs, "don't say that!"

Vader raises the knife over his head, swaying like a wounded bear.

My voice cries out on its own: "Vader! Don't!"

Vader stops. When he looks at me, his face is so distorted with anguish that I shrink back.

The knife drops from his hand.

Moeder clutches me to her as he climbs up the stairs. My face pressed into her salty bodice, I seek out the painting. Mijnheer Gootman watches me from the floor, his single eye calmly seeing.

Chapter 9

Three days have passed since my shaming before Carel the Handsome, and the sting of it still has not lessened. I still feel ill when I remember the startled look on Carel's face after Vader insulted him. The thought of it makes me blush even now, as I maintain the pose in which Neel has positioned me before the window. Neel has put me here for the light, though thankfully there is not much of it shining through the thick panes of wavy glass. It is late morning but such a cloudy day in March that the canal outside looks as black as a bog, matching my mood. I don't see how Neel can work. There is no room. Since Vader has locked himself up in his studio again, Neel must paint downstairs in the front room, in a space already overcrowded by the printing press with its windmill-like crank and the square bulk of my four-poster bed. With the addition of Neel's easel, stool, and workbench, we are as penned in as geese to be fattened for market—geese with an irritating view of Vader's unsold paintings on the walls, that is.

Neel puts down his brush. "Cornelia, you are thrashing around like a worm under a boot. I cannot paint."

I pull out of the pose, stretch my arms, then scratch under my bodice. "How can you expect me to stay twisted that way?" I am doing him a favor, modeling for him. I am also trying to draw his attention away from Vader, who has become very secretive ever since Carel rejected Vader's painting several days ago. He does not even allow his dear rump-kissing Neel into his studio. When Vader leaves, he throws a drape over the canvas he is working on. If he's in, he makes me set his tray outside his room when I bring him his meals. The old fox is up to something. I only hope he does not lose his last remaining student while he is at it. Neel is loyal, but even rump kissers have only so much patience.

"What you call 'twisting,'" Neel says, "we painters call *contrapposto.*" He sits back on his stool.

"I know what contrapposto is," I say, not willing to be outshone by a mere apprentice. Just because I have not been encouraged to paint by my vader does not mean I know nothing about it. "Leonardo da Vinci used it in all his works. He thought that arranging his figures on a curving axis added life to his compositions."

As a child, I would sneak upstairs when Moeder was sleeping and Vader was away to look at a certain drawing on the wall of a woman and her little son holding a lamb—a sketch, I found out later, Vader had made from a copy of a da Vinci painting he had seen. In just a few strokes of his pen, Vader had captured the woman's amused adoration for her child as she reached out to him. How I had envied that child. If only Vader would reach out to me that way.

No matter now. I push open the window a crack and cold air rushes in, fluttering my cap strings. I close it quickly, then with a sigh, look longingly at my bed, where behind the pulled curtains my new book awaits. Yesterday I had been able to make good use of a trip to the apothecary for linseed oil for Vader by stopping at the bookseller's shop to exchange my old book. Now, if only I could just sneak off to read.

"Your vader used contrapposto most intriguingly, I think, in his last *Bathsheba*," Neel is saying. He glances at me as if he has said too much. "In many other paintings, too," he adds quickly.

"I don't remember him doing a Bathsheba." I think of the story in the Bible of the woman who must choose between becoming the lover of rich King David and staying faithful to her lowly soldier husband who is never at home. It seems such an obvious outcome: go with the king.

I do not know the painting he speaks of, but I also do not care. "Vader's work is not of interest to me."

Neel crosses his arms and smiles gently as if he does not believe me.

His calmness provokes me. "It would be different if he painted in a more popular style," I say with heat. "He can, too, when he wants."

I point to a picture on the wall of Titus's mother, Saskia, crowned with flowers and holding a flower wand. The surfaces in the painting are perfectly smooth, and the colors clear and bright. "Vader could sell that one, just like that." I snap my fingers. "But would he ever dream of parting with his precious Saskia?"

"You cannot blame your vader for not wanting to sell a painting of his wife, Cornelia."

"Especially not of dearest Saskia. Let us all bow down and worship her." Why am I such a bitter old lemon when Neel is about? Why doesn't he just tell me to seal my vicious lips?

He gets up from his stool and calmly squeezes some red paint from a tied-up pig bladder onto his palette. "Are there not plenty of paintings around here with your mother as a model as well?"

"Yes. Dark, globby, frightening ones."

He waits, his long face calm with patience. If he would only say something, I would shut my hateful mouth. But no, he just stares at me with those maddeningly sympathetic eyes.

"You have seen that one in the entranceway of my moeder wading in the river in but a shift. It is pulled up past her knees! At least the prostitutes in the park across the street are smart enough to collect a few guilders before baring their legs." I look for him to flinch.

Unruffled, he mixes the dab of red paint with some white. "It is a beautiful painting, Cornelia."

"Beautiful! How would you like to have your moeder painted in her shift?"

"It would make a terrible picture," he says simply. "My moeder was not handsome."

"That's an uncharitable thing to say."

"I state the truth. It has nothing to do with my moeder's worth as a person. She was not especially beautiful on the outside, but her kindness shone from within. I cannot count how many neighbors she nursed during the last visitation of the plague, without hesitation or complaint. Maybe I am wrong. Maybe she would be a good subject for a portrait, though . . ."

I reopen the window and stick my head into the chilly air. "Lucky you," I say, concentrating on the moeder duck floating by with her ducklings, on the peeling blue paint of the boat moored on the canal, on the pale buds on the linden branches hanging over the black water—anything to shut out the memory pushing at the edge of my mind. "With such a perfect life at home, I'm surprised you ever left Dordrecht."

There is sadness in Neel's brown eyes when I pull back into the room, but he says nothing further, making me feel like even more of a beast.

"Here." I slam the window shut and twist myself into the position I had held earlier, then make a bored face. "Is this how you wished me to stand? Let's just get this done."

"Hardly conducive to one's muse," Neel murmurs with a frown, but he gets up from his stool. He is painting in silence when a knock sounds at the door.

My heart leaps into my throat. The peat merchant has

come to cut off our credit. Or perhaps it is that terrible man whose hair, face, and clothes are as oily as if they'd been stewed in butter—the bill collector—and Neel is standing right here. I shall not answer.

But what if the bill collector starts yelling, like last time? Housewives up and down the street came out to stare. Boaters paused on the canal. Everyone was poised for the show, and Vader granted them one, by opening the window and heaving out a maggoty cabbage. The Oily One had no trouble collecting witnesses when he made his report to the constable. Cost us five guilders in fines.

The knocking comes again.

Neel pulls back from the canvas. "I can wait, Cornelia."

He wipes his brush as I go to the tiny entrance hall and open the door.

Titus jumps at me. "Boo!"

"You horrible brat!" I swat at him. "Why did you do that?" I leave him laughing. "I was modeling," I call over my shoulder. "Why have you been gone so long?"

He nods to Neel, then grins at me. "Some artist's model you are, Cornelia, keeping your clothes on."

Neel's face hardens. "That is not funny, Titus."

"Sorry, old man, it was just a stupid jest." Titus raises his brows at me as if to get my support, but I cannot smile. His remark has wounded me deeply.

Titus laughs uneasily. "Worry Bird, you know I was joking. I'm sorry, it was crude of me."

I fight off the sick feeling in my stomach. Why am I taking this jest so hard? "It doesn't matter."

Neel watches me with concern, making me feel even more unsettled, as Titus leans against the printing press and looks up at the ceiling. "Where is Vader?"

"Guess," I say stoutly, glad to be on to another subject.

"I heard he took a painting to Gerrit van Uylenburgh the other day."

"How did you know?" I glance at Neel. It would not do for him to know what a failure that excursion was.

Titus pushes on one of the wooden arms of the press's crank, causing the printing cylinder to slowly turn. "Gerrit Hendrickszoon came to dinner yesterday," he says, using van Uylenburgh's familiar name as if they had been cronies since the cradle. "He said he has a potential buyer."

"He does?" I remember Neel's presence and even out the tone of my voice. "Oh, well, I guess I am a little surprised. Van Uylenburgh did not see the painting, but I suppose Vader's reputation is enough to go on."

"Gerrit Hendrickszoon said the boy told him about it." Titus puts his finger to the printing cylinder, then pulls it away, inky. "Nicolaes Bruyningh's nephew."

I make my voice light and unconcerned. "His name is Carel, I think."

Neel looks up.

I am furious to find myself blushing.

"You would not remember Nicolaes Bruyningh," Titus says,

wiping his finger underneath the press, "but I do. He sat for Vader back in the days Vader was friends with the Stadholder. Nicolaes must have been younger than I am now—about Neel's age, twenty-one, twenty-two. Entertained everyone in the house. Stories? The man was a wit. I worshipped him. His nephew would be lucky if he was anything like him."

Neel is watching me.

"Where is Magdalena?" I ask Titus.

"Home, interviewing a maid. Her old one left her last week. I never knew it was such a chore to keep a servant—evidently they leave on the slightest whim. Magdalena is always having to replace them."

I have met Magdalena only twice, once fleetingly on the street when I was out buying bacon with Titus, the other at her wedding, just before the predicant commenced reading the vows, but I cannot help but wonder how much of Magdalena's maid problem lies with her and how much with the maids. She was not exactly friendly to me, though with my poor pedigree, what person of quality would be? Even though Titus's moeder was kin to Magdalena's family, with Vader dirtying the waters, it is a miracle they allowed Titus to marry her—a testament to Titus's great charm.

"When is she coming here?" I ask.

"Oh, she'll be along eventually. She is busy just yet, giving trade to every purveyor of fine goods in Amsterdam. Now that there is a new man in the house, it seems there must be a complete collection of new tapestries, linens, and furniture, too."

"How do you afford—" I break off, glancing at Neel, who is mixing more white into the umber on his palette.

"The van Loos have more money than they know what to do with." Titus pushes away from the press, his eyes bright. "You wouldn't believe it, Neeltje. I haven't slept in the same set of sheets yet. I think they must have hundreds."

"Titus?" It is Vader, at the top of the stairs. "Do I hear your voice? Titus?" Vader tramps down the stairs. Though it has been only seventeen days since Titus's last visit, Vader clamps Titus to him now has as if Titus were the prodigal son, fresh from the pigpen.

"Vader," Titus gasps when he can get a breath. "How are you?"

"Good, son," Vader says in his throaty voice. "Good."

We are as packed in the room as herring in a jar. I open the window again just to breathe. In floats a ridiculously jaunty tune from the carillon of the Westerkerk, marking a damp gray noon.

"Vader," Titus says, "I heard you took a picture to Gerrit Hendrickszoon."

Vader lets him go. "How did you know?" He frowns at me as if I have revealed our failed mission.

"He came to dinner," Titus says. "But that is not my news. Vader—he has a possible buyer."

Vader's white brows draw together. "How can the van Uylenburgh whelp have a buyer? He did not even see the painting."

"The Bruyningh boy told him about the picture."

"Bruyningh," Vader says. He looks as if he's trying to decide something, then notices me. "Cornelia, quit peeping outside like a mouse from its hole and shut that window. That damned tune is killing me."

"You are famous enough that people do not have to see your work," Titus says to Vader as I pull inside with a shamed glance at Neel, though he is gazing intently at his canvas as if he had not heard Vader treat me like a child. "If they learn that something of yours is new on the market, they are interested."

I wish to roll my eyes. This load of ox manure about Vader's fame grows smellier with each telling.

"Well," Vader says, "I am no longer interested in selling it."

"Vader!" Titus exclaims.

Vader shuffles around the printing press, shoves open the curtains to my bed, and eases himself down. I am thankful that I had the foresight to hide my new book under my pillow. "The painting does not say what I meant for it to say. It needs further work."

"Oh, Vader," Titus says, "that painting was perfectly fine. If someone wants it, sell it. You can paint others."

Vader winces.

I study Titus to see if he catches Vader's veiled look of hurt. I notice Neel watching Titus, too.

"Forget about that for now," Titus says. "Look what I brought." From the deep pockets of his new cassock, he pulls two green-waxed balls of Edam and sets them on the table. "Herbed. Your favorite, Vader."

"Oh." Vader sighs, then smiles.

Titus digs again and brings out a set of silver candlestick holders. The dim light coming through the window is enough to set off the delicate flowers etched into the shining metal. "Come here, Cornelia."

I slip past the clutter to his side. "Whose are those?"

Titus holds them out to me. "Yours."

"Candlestick holders?"

"Magdalena's vader was the head of the silversmiths' guild. They have this sort of thing sitting around all over their house."

"But aren't they Magdalena's?"

Titus laughs. "They're mine to give. Everything of Magdalena's is mine to give. Here, take them."

The candlestick holders are heavy—much silver must be in them. How many guilders could a fine pair such as these fetch? Like the maid in the tale who dreams on the way to the market of the things she can buy with her eggs, my brain races with plans. I could purchase bread to make me look less gaunt and young; a lilac satin bodice to attract a suitor; pearl earrings to hint at my wealth, so when I did attract a suitor, he'd be good and rich. We have not resorted yet to stealing, at least not that I know of, but stranger things have happened in the house of van Rijn.

"Give them back, Cornelia," Vader says.

"But they're my gift to her, Vader."

"Give them back, Cornelia. Believe me," he says pointedly, "take things that aren't yours, and it always comes back to haunt you."

Titus takes back the candlestick holders with a frown. "Get dressed, Vader. I am taking us to the inn for a bite."

Vader shakes his head. "Too expensive."

"No trouble." Titus jingles his pockets. "You come, too, Neel."

"Thank you," Neel says, "but I should be going. You go on, Cornelia. I will clean up my brushes."

"Vader," Titus says, "run to the back room and change into your cassock. You cannot wear that old paint-spattered dressing gown out on the street."

He usually does, I think.

Vader reaches under my pillow. He holds up my book. "What is this?"

Titus squints at the cover as I rush around the furniture. "I believe," he says, "it is a book called *Maidenly Virtues: The Young Woman's Guide to Comportment.*"

I lean over Vader and grab it. My face burns as I stuff it back under my pillow.

"Oh ho," says Titus, "which virtues do you wish to acquire, Bird?"

Even Neel smiles. I shall murder them all.

Vader pushes himself up slowly from the bed. "Leave the girl alone," he says, then totters out of the room.

"Cornelia," Titus whispers as soon as Vader is gone, "if Vader will not bring that picture to Gerrit Hendrickszoon, you must. Gerrit Hendrickszoon said this is a buyer with a deep purse."

I jerk my bed curtains closed. He makes sport of me, then expects me to risk making a fool of myself before Carel? "You cannot be serious," I say with heat.

"Oh, yes, Bird, I can, and the sooner the better, while the buyer is interested. You must go tomorrow."

"Tomorrow!" Panic erases my pique. "How?" I know little of the business end of art. It is the painting I have always wished to do, not the dealing.

Titus pats me on the head. "You are a resourceful girl. You will think of a way."

"But—but Vader has already taken it off the stretchers."

"All the easier for you to carry it."

Neel looks at us over his shoulder as he wipes his brush with a rag. I think of the Christ in Vader's *Peter Denying Christ*, gazing over his shoulder at Peter, disappointed acceptance writ all over his face. Neel wears the same expression.

"Very well," I say firmly, startling even myself. "I shall do it." Titus and I don't need Neel's acceptance. Who is he to judge us? He has not lived his life in the shadow of Vader's instability.

Vader comes back in his cassock, grinning. "Are we ready, then?"

"As soon as I shave you, Vader," says Titus with a wink at me. "You are as furry as a fox."

"I should be glad for you to shave me. Cornelia shaved me last time."

Titus raises his sleek brows. "You shaved him?"

"Not willingly," I grumble.

"I cannot imagine this. Did she leave you as nicked up as an executioner's block?"

I wait for Vader to complain but all he says is, "You can shave me, son."

He missed an opportunity to compare me unfavorably to Titus? Perhaps the old man is failing after all.

But soon his sagging cheeks are freshly naked and we leave for the inn. For the moment, the thought of tucking into a glistening joint of meat after weeks of nothing but dry cheese and watery soup outweighs all cares about Neel's possible disappointment in me and the risk of exposing myself before Carel if I peddle Vader's picture. Still, my watering mouth does not chase away one last question: just what things had Vader taken that were not his?

Chapter 10

The Anatomy Lesson of Dr. Jan Deyman.

1656. Canvas.

My legs are tired. If you step on a crack, you break your moeder's back, but Moeder is walking fast and I can hardly hop quickly enough from brick to brick in my clompen. It is November and my breath comes out in clouds in the cold air.

"Are we almost there, Moeder?" I know it is silly for an eight-year-old to jump cracks, but I do it anyhow. You have to be nimble to do it in clompen because they slip on the bricks. I have not stepped on a crack since we left home.

"Two more canals to cross," she says.

My hop sends me into the empty basket that swings on Moeder's arm.

"Careful, puss."

I can see her breath, too, and her nose and cheeks are red from the cold. It is freezing outside but it is better than staying at home, where the picture of Mijnheer Gootman still lies on the front-room floor though it has been a week since the men brought it back from the Town Hall.

"Why do we have to go to this baker?" I ask. "I like our baker on the Rozengracht. Mijnheer Frankrijk puts extra sugar on the buns if you ask him."

"This baker is much better," Moeder says.

I keep hopping but my tiptoes hurt. Finally Moeder turns into a shop. I jump inside the door onto the smooth black and white tiles on the floor. I can walk anywhere I want in here. Cracks between tiles don't count.

Moeder twists the red beads hidden under her gauze neckcloth and orders two loaves of bread from the baker, who is covered with flour from his frizzy white hair to his round-toed shoes. I push my cape off my arms. It is hot in here after the cold outside, but it smells good, like baking bread. I look on the shelves for the fancy iced cakes shaped like lambs or ducks or rabbits, but there are none. Someone must have already bought them.

The baker gives Moeder the bread. She fits it into her basket. "And a dozen currant buns, please."

I look at her in surprise. Has Vader sold a painting? We are going to eat like kings!

"Four stuivers, please," the baker says.

Moeder tucks away the buns. "Could you please put that on my bill?"

The baker's smile goes away.

"I ran out today without a single stuiver," she says. "Isn't that ridiculous? I shall return on Friday to pay."

The baker's voice is not nice. "Whom shall I record on the bill?"

Moeder touches her beads. "Hendrickje Stoffels."

I look at Moeder. Why doesn't she say that she's the wife of Rembrandt van Rijn? Vader is famous. He knows rich people.

"We live at 4 Breestraat."

What is wrong with her? That was our old address. We moved four years ago. I tug at her elbow.

"Good day, mijnheer." She grabs my hand and pulls me out of the bakery. I'm so surprised I forget to jump the cracks. When I remember, it's too late.

"Oh!"

"What's wrong?" She gives me a bun before I can answer. "Here."

I look at the bun. It's not even de noen. She always makes me wait until de noen to eat after we have had breakfast.

"Go ahead. Eat it."

I take a bite. Bah! Moeder was wrong. This bun is not as good as the buns from the other bakery; it is dry and hardly sweet. I don't wait to empty my mouth to tell her the bad news.

"Shhh, puss," she says. "I am trying to find our way."

The houses here are different from our neighborhood. Taller. Cleaner. "Where are we?" When I look up at my moeder, there are tears in her eyes.

She wipes her eyes when she sees me looking. "It's from the cold." She smiles. "How would you like to see the biggest house in Amsterdam?"

I nod yes, though I don't want to. I want to go home.

"It's on the Kloveniersburgwal," Moeder says. "Isn't that a funny name?"

"Klo-Klov—"

"Kloveniersburgwal. You had better learn it, puss. It is the name of

money." Her voice is happy, but her smile goes away when she turns to look around.

"Here," she says after we walk a minute, "this is the passage."

We are hurrying so fast I cannot eat my bun. We come to a canal. It is much wider than ours, with beautiful painted boats on it, and there are big trees, their bare arms reaching into the cloudy sky. A shiny green carriage drawn by six white horses clatters by. I stare at it in wonder. Carriages drawn by six matched horses don't come down the Rozengracht.

"How much farther?"

"Just a few more houses—it is right up there. We are on the Kloveniersburgwal now. Isn't it pretty here?" She keeps her face pointed ahead, even though there is a boy with pretty gold hair watching us from the porch next to us. Someone opens the door to the house and pulls him inside.

Moeder seems not to have seen him. "You will like this mansion," she says lightly. "For two years I have watched it rise out of the ground. It belongs to the Trip family. Your vader is painting the portraits of the Trippen for it—how do you like that?"

I nod as if I like it, though I hope they don't send the picture back like they did from the Town Hall. Since then, many days Vader goes away in the morning and comes back at nighttime smelling of ale.

I stumble on a cobblestone and drop my bun. When I open my mouth to protest, I see Moeder staring at something down the street.

"Moeder?"

She puts her hand to her hidden beads with a little cry, but I see nothing different, just a group of men in black hats and capes, coming down the walkway like you see everywhere in Amsterdam.

She pulls me away from the dropped bun. We start running in the other direction. We run past one big building and another, my clompen slipping on the bricks, to the end of the street, where there is a big castle with five pointy-topped towers.

"What is this place?" My cap tips off my head as I look up at the main door. A giant could fit through it.

Moeder doesn't answer, just throws open the door, her basket banging against the wood, and tugs me inside, my cap flapping. The group of men passes by. One of them looks over his shoulder at us, his golden curls under his big black hat catching on his collar. I wriggle out of Moeder's grip to see him better. Could it be—is it my gold mustache man? I hope it is him so I can ask Moeder who he is. I tap my lips in our signal, but before he can tap back, Moeder pulls me into the dark and leans against the wall, clutching her basket.

"Moeder, I wanted to see! Where are we?"

She doesn't answer for a moment. When she does, she is out of breath. "The Weighing House."

"It's all dark. Why are we here?" Now I will never know if it was him.

I can hear her swallow between breaths. "I wanted to show . . . your vader did a painting . . ."

"May I help you?"

Moeder screams.

A bent old man holding a broom steps into the strip of light from the half-closed door.

"Sorry, mevrouw! I did not mean to scare you." He scratches at one of the white bunches of hair curled over each ear. He smells of bacon and dust.

"I am fine." Moeder pats at her beads. She is still breathing hard. "I am the . . . wife of Rembrandt van Rijn." She pushes me forward. "I have brought my daughter . . . to see his picture of Dr. Deyman's anatomy lesson."

"Ah, the famous painting."

Moeder nods.

He looks at me, then raises his droopy white brows at her. "The little girl . . . ?"

Moeder opens her mouth, then closes it. "I did not think of that. I was remembering what a success . . . Never mind." She turns to go. "Come, Cornelia."

"But—you brought me in here to see it." I like Vader's paintings. Sometimes the people in them are so real they almost talk to me. I think they must know I am Vader's daughter.

Moeder rubs at her neck. "A quick look, then."

Tap, step. Tap, step. The old man uses his broom as a staff as he leads us up the stone staircase. "I know your husband," he says. "I met him when he was doing the picture, though I'd heard of him before. Everyone has heard of the famous Rembrandt."

"Yes," Moeder murmurs.

"They say he has a bit of devilment in him, but he always had a smile and a nod for me."

We reach the top of the steps, then head down a dark hall. The tapping of the old man's broom handle echoes from the ceiling.

"I thought I remembered hearing Rembrandt lost his wife the year he did that painting that caused all the commotion, the picture of Captain Banning Cocq's company."

"That was his first wife," Moeder says.

"Ohhh. Excuse me, mevrouw. I don't believe I had heard he had remarried, but my memory's gone tricky. You could tell me anything and I would forget it before de noen the next day. Congratulations, mevrouw."

Moeder murmurs something.

The tapping stops. There is a jangle of keys, then the creaking of a hinge. A strong smell, even sharper than Vader's paints, bites the inside of my nose as I step inside a dark room.

"Moeder, what stinks?"

"They do anatomies in here, little miss," says the man. "Mevrouw, are you sure we should—"

I hear the rustle of Moeder's bodice as she looks behind her. "Yes. Yes. But quickly, please."

My nose runs as we wait for the man to push back the shutters at the windows with his broom handle. When the light pours in, I can see wooden seats all around, in rows that go down like steps. I follow Moeder's stare to a big painting on the wall. I walk underneath it, my clompen clacking on the tile.

The picture is of men gathered around another man, who is lying on a table. The man on the table has big bare feet, pointed right at me, almost coming out of the picture, and they are dirty. There is a cloth across his legs, but he is bare, all bare, and his stomach is all black.

No, it's not black, it's a big hole. A big, big hole. His insides have been scooped out like a roasting hen's.

"Thank you, mijnheer," Moeder says. "We must go now. Come, Neeltje."

I cannot move. Why have they taken out his insides? Insides aren't supposed to come out. They don't want to come out, they want to stay inside and hide. If they get out, people will know bad things about you, secret things. You have to keep them hidden.

"Neeltje, please!"

Even dead, with his insides let loose, the hollow man's face is unhappy under the mop of thick rosy hair hanging over his forehead.

Wait.

No.

That is not rose-colored hair, parted and pushed down from the top of his head; it is the hollow man's own dead flesh. They have cut open his head and are looking inside.

"They're not supposed to look in there! It's supposed to stay inside! No one is to see it."

"Don't cry, schaapje," the old man says. "There now, little maid."

But when I turn around to protest that I am not crying, I see he is not talking to me.

He is speaking to Moeder.

Chapter 11

It is a rare bright day in March. The sun shines into the water of the canal, giving it the brown and cloudy look of beef broth. I slog over van Uylenburgh's bridge with Vader's quickly unfurling canvas. What a sight I must be—the canvas is as heavy as a calf and as hard to hold as one, too, and the linen strips I hastily wrapped around it before I stole it out of the house are unwinding like bandages from a neglected wound. Curse you, Titus, for suggesting I bring it here. We do not need the money this badly. I would rather starve than have Carel come to the door and find the madman's daughter wrestling with this flapping beast. A well-bred girl my age is supposed to trip daintily down the street with her maid by her side, not haul ungainly wares across town like a dockworker.

I knock, praying for the maid to answer or another student or even van Uylenburgh himself—anyone but Carel.

The door creaks open on rusty hinges. Carel Bruyningh stands in the entrance in his shirtsleeves. "Yes?"

The minute I see his handsome face, I know I was the dullest of simpletons to think that if I brushed my hair, put on a clean cap and collar, and cleansed my teeth with a piece of straw, I would be presentable enough for the likes of him.

"I am Cornelia, daughter of—"

"I know who you are."

I hold back my groan. Of course he does. Everyone knows the daughters of madmen and criminals.

Well, now that I have made a sight of myself and ruined the chance I never had with him anyway, I might as well get on with business. "My brother said Mijnheer van Uylenburgh had a buyer for this picture."

"Here, that must be heavy."

He is taller than me—Titus's height, but more well muscled. I dare not look at his golden curls as he takes the canvas from my arms, but oh, I can smell him. Salty bread, green leaves, and soap. I breathe deeply.

"Are you well?" he asks.

A startled snort escapes me. "Yes."

"I thought maybe you had a cold."

"No. I am fine." Why can I not behave like a normal girl? Why must I always be my vader's coarse daughter? I might as well scratch my armpits and spit.

He folds back a corner of the canvas that has flopped open. "Which picture is this?" He speaks as if we were two respectable people in the habit of discussing art.

I compose my voice. "It is a family group, as Mijnheer van Uylenburgh requested for his buyer."

"Really?" He catches at the canvas as it slithers onto the stoop. "Van Uylenburgh found someone?" he says, scrambling to pick it up.

The painting appears not to have been hurt. I bob in a flustered curtsy. I am going to kill Titus. "I am sorry to trouble you. I must have misunderstood. It must have been another dealer—"

"Hello?" It's a man's voice. "Is that Rembrandt's girl?"

Gerrit van Uylenburgh comes to the doorway. Without his large hat, he is a whole other creature, like a snail without its shell. He is just a mite of a man, with dark-lashed blue eyes, a turned-up nose, and little hair on his narrow head. What remains of his locks starts just above his ears and hangs to his shoulders in a wispy black veil.

"Is this the family group Titus was telling me about?" he says.

Titus, the brother I'm going to murder? "Yes, mijnheer."

"Come in. Let me see this thing. It was a private deal," he tells Carel when he sees Carel's look of confusion.

Silently cursing Titus, I step inside the entrance hall and look around as Carel lets the canvas slump to the floor and van Uylenburgh gets on his knees to examine it. Though the blue and white floor tiles glisten and the dark wood of the walls gleams, the air seethes with the scent of boiling mutton and onions. Through this sheep-scented miasma, I see the walls are hung with paintings of historical subjects rendered in smooth, bright colors. They will sell fast, no doubt. From what Titus tells me, such paintings are all the rage, though to me, they are as empty of emotion as a China plate. In spite of all their roughness, I prefer Vader's paintings—perhaps because of it. Somehow, through those slashes of paint, the inner person comes to the surface. How does Vader do it? How does he make Baby van Roop and all the love he feels for his moeder—the same deep love Titus feels for Vader—come alive in dabs of pigment arranged on the canvas at my feet?

I notice Carel watching me. Shame, then anger wells up inside me. I must be a curiosity to him, like the arm in the jar in Vader's studio.

Gerrit van Uylenburgh stands up. "I saw you at the wedding," he says, brushing off the knees of his black breeches. "You are all grown up now. How old are you?"

"Almost fourteen." Just give me the money and I shall leave.

He nods. "Well, I suppose the old man keeps you busy."

"Yes, mijnheer."

"He hasn't changed a bit, I see. Does what he pleases when he pleases."

"Yes, mijnheer." I glance at the door.

"Well, we aren't here to disparage your father, are we?" He fluffs back the remains of his hair. "As I told Titus, I might have a buyer for this piece. How much does your vader ask?"

I look at him stupidly. "I can't say."

"He sent you here with a painting to sell and you don't know the price?"

Tears of frustration burn at my throat. It was all I could do to lug the canvas out of the house while Vader was on a walk along the river. I was so occupied with getting away with the painting while not sweating onto the fresh cap I had donned in case I saw Carel that I had not thought of the selling price.

"Cagey as ever—my vader warned me about him," van Uylenburgh says. "Doesn't want to limit his offer, does he? Well, this kind of rough thing doesn't fetch much, no matter what kind of game your vader wants to play. But the buyer did ask specifically for this picture."

"May I ask," I say, "who it is?" Titus would want to know.

"He wishes to remain anonymous." Van Uylenburgh glances at Carel. "At least until after the purchase is made. Then he will reveal himself." He holds open the door. "I shall send word of his offer. Thank you for bringing the painting. It must have been a beast to carry."

I cannot move. As eager as I was for *buchts*, I had not thought of the possibility of returning home without any. Stupid! Had I not heard Vader complain a thousand times how slow buyers were to pay? Now I have nothing with which to calm Vader's temper when he finds the picture missing.

"I have got other clients coming soon." Van Uylenburgh looks over my head in case I had not caught his meaning.

"*Dank u wel.*" I bob my good-bye and hasten away.

Outside, the fishy smell of the canal quickly overtakes the sheepy odor of the house of van Uylenburgh. I am thinking how Vader is going to roar, when I hear someone call, "Cornelia!"

Carel strides toward me, the tassels of his collar bouncing on his taut chest. He has run out without his cassock. I touch my cap, then my throat. Why had I not worn Moeder's red beads? I had them in my hand, but I am so stupid about them. I've done nothing wrong, I can wear them all I want. Now I look but plain and young.

"I'm glad your vader's picture has a buyer," he says.

Vader again. I start walking along the canal.

He falls in stride beside me. "I could not get it out of my mind after I saw it," he says. "It was almost as if you could feel what was inside of each person."

I glance at him.

He looks over his shoulder. "I had to get out of there. I am apprenticed to Ferdinand Bol, who has got a studio in van Uylenburgh's house, but van Uylenburgh thinks I am his errand boy. He works me to the bone if I let him." When he smiles, the sunlight catches his golden lashes. His eyes are the bright blue of a jay's wing.

My gaze dives for the bricks of the walkway. "How soon will van Uylenburgh pay? Not that it matters."

"It might be weeks. Buyers are notorious for not paying until their arms are twisted. I don't know who this one is—some are worse than others. The richer they are, the slower they pay."

"That's not fair."

"That is the way it is." We stop at the bridge. A brisk

March wind blows his blond curls off his forehead. His skin is tawny, almost as golden as his hair. At that moment, the death bells of the Westerkerk sound, their deep ringing almost as loud at this remove as at home.

"Someone has died again," he says.

I notice the sprinkling of golden freckles on his face when he frowns. "Yes."

"Does it seem to you that they have been ringing more than usual these days?"

I thought only I noticed them. "Are they?"

"I don't know. I suppose I could count them. I don't remember them going so often, not since the beginning of . . ." He scowls and takes a breath.

His frown dissolves like sunlight in the murky water of the canal. "Guess what?" he says, smiling. "I know someone who has met you."

Something twists in my stomach. Has someone been saying bad things again about my family? "Who?" I say, too fast.

He holds up his hands in innocence. "Just my uncle! I saw him at the shipyard after you came to van Uylenburgh's last week. He said he knows you."

"He does?" Carel has talked about me to his uncle? I pull my cap down over my ears. I should have taken the time to wash my hair. I should have ironed my apron. I should have worn the beads. I should have done everything differently. "I must have been too young when we met—I don't remember him. But Titus does."

Carel laughs. "You must have been the freshest infant. Uncle Nicolaes is a hard one to forget. He's quite charming."

We walk to the top of the bridge. Carel picks up a stone and drops it into the canal. We watch the rings spread across the water.

"So you want to be a painter?" I ask.

"I have known it since I was little. After Vader would take me to our shipyard, I would come home and draw ships all over his ledgers. He didn't thank me for that."

"I suppose not!"

"I did make a mess of those ledgers. But they were some pretty good ships." He smiles when I laugh.

"My vader said painting was not a profession worthy of someone of our sort," he says. "But I am not doing it for the money. The family business will provide me with enough of that."

I frown at the windmill on its mound at the end of the street, its white cloth sails turning briskly in the same breeze that is ruffling Carel's curls. Handsome and rich. Why is it that those who least need more blessings are the ones who get them?

"I think I shall be admitted to the guild early," he says. "At least I hope so. My masterpiece is nearly ready. Not bad for a sixteen-year-old."

Sixteen. Two years older than me. Two years from now, both of us will be of marrying age.

"What kind do you do?" I ask.

"Kind?"

"Of painting—still life, landscape, genre?"

"Oh. Still life. I can do a half-peeled lemon that makes you think you should finish peeling it. I do good bread, too—do not laugh!"

"I am not," I say, laughing.

"It is glass that is tough. I am just figuring out how to capture light on the surface. It's very difficult, you know."

"Light is always the hardest thing to get right. We take it for granted, but in painting, it is everything."

"True, light does affect everything—color, shape, depth." He lays his hand on the stone wall of the bridge. The sunshine lights up the tiny golden hairs on his knuckles. "This same hand held just so would be painted differently depending on whether the scene was indoors or out. If outside, the time of day and amount of shade would affect it. If inside, whether it was lit by daylight or candle. One hand—many kinds of light."

"My vader once painted a hand with candlelight shining *through* it. You could faintly see the bones within."

He stares at me. "That is brilliant. Was it beautiful?"

I lean over to look at the water. "Actually, it was frightening."

"Frightening?"

"It reminds you that there is a whole other being inside you."

I can feel him watching me as I push away from the wall.

"I have never talked to a girl about such things," he says, following me down the slope of the bridge. "The girls I'm introduced to know nothing but gloves and gowns and necklaces. You know about things that matter."

I risk pausing to look back at him. Our eyes meet. We glance away quickly, but when we resume walking, the air around us is different. Lighter. Though merchants and maids and housewives rush by us, their capes snapping in the wind, we float forward in our own special bubble.

We come to the end of the bridge. "I have to go back," he says.

I cannot speak. Anything I say can burst our delicate sphere.

"We shall talk again," he says.

I listen to his footsteps on the bricks until I hear them no more, then run, holding in great whoops of joy.

Neel is in the crowded front room, one of Vader's straw figures before his canvas. "There you are. Your vader has been searching all over for you."

"Hello, Neel!" I want to kiss his sober old face. I hang my cloak on a peg and dance toward the kitchen.

Neel follows. "Mijnheer's family portrait is missing. The one Titus claimed yesterday to have a buyer for."

My breath stops. "Does Vader know it is gone?"

"No, I don't think so. Cornelia, tell me you do not know where it has gone."

Relief pours through my veins. "Hungry for some cheese,

Neel?" I open a crock, searching for one of those balls of Edam Titus had brought.

"Tell me you did not listen to Titus. That painting is worth more than just some guilders."

I tip the lid of another crock. "How much *is* it worth, do you think?"

"Do you not understand? Its worth cannot be measured by gold."

"Neel, please, calm yourself. They'll cart you off to the Dolhuis." I chuckle at the thought of Serious Neel surrounded by the raving inmates of the asylum.

"This is no jest, Cornelia. That picture should never be bought or sold. It is bigger than that."

"Nothing is bigger than money."

"You don't know what you're saying." Neel crosses his arms as I brush by him to look on a shelf. "You would do well to be more of your father's daughter."

Thank you, Neel Suythof, for thinking I am *not* like my vader. But when I turn around, he looks so serious that I laugh. "I suppose you, too, believe it was painted by God."

"Have you really looked at that painting, Cornelia?"

I frown. If only he knew how much I had. "Yes."

"How else would you explain the truth of emotion in that picture? Is it so impossible for God to have guided him? Have you another explanation?"

I pull a cloth off a lump next to the spice grater. "Ah, here's the cheese! Would you—"

Neel is gone.

Oh, well, I think as I pare the green rind off a wedge I have cut. I shall eat alone. There is more for me this way. But the cheese loses its savor as I chew it, alone in the damp kitchen. How *does* one explain how Vader perfectly captured a child's love for his parent on canvas? It seems beyond a regular mortal, let alone one as gruff and crude and palsied as Vader. How did he do it?

Chapter 12

It has been more than a week since my walk with Carel, but at the moment, fear has driven any warm and happy thoughts of him as deeply underground as the piles that keep every building in Amsterdam from sinking into the marshy soil. Vader has been vile tempered since breakfast and I know not why, but if he discovers that his painting is missing in such a mood, objects will fly.

To this end, I am in the attic, choking on dust and the tarry smell of the roof beams as I skirt past chests and straw figures and strange objects covered with cloths. I want not to uncover things if I don't have to—it is like disturbing a grave. Releasing ghosts. I have avoided this attic for many a year, and I have had no reason to come here. It is Vader's storeroom. His rubbish. The *drek* he cannot use in his studio, he drags across the landing into here. But there are paintings in here, I know. I have seen them, long ago. I need one now. If I am lucky, I can find a rolled-up one to substitute for the family group I have taken to van Uylenburgh. I can put it in his studio where the other one was. It is a miracle Vader has not missed it already, perhaps due to his work on his mysterious project. Or could it be that his lack of notice is more evidence of his failing mind?

There is something that looks to be a roll of canvas on the floor. I push it with my foot, lifting dust, but it does not come undone. Several strings bind it along its length.

The floorboard creaks behind me.

I gasp. "Hello?"

Tijger strolls in, calm as a king though his faded orange legs are bowed with age.

"You." I pick him up. He weighs less than dust. "You gave me a fright."

He regards me, unconcerned.

I put him down. My heart beating in my ears, I bend down to peel back an edge of the canvas.

A silky fringe falls against my hand. There are swirls of raw sienna and sable against rich vermilion.

A carpet. What was I so afraid of?

I sit back on my heels and sigh.

"Cornelia."

I whirl around. Neel is standing in the doorway.

The man blows about as silently as duck down. "What do you want?"

"I am looking for your vader."

I walk briskly toward him, forcing him to back onto the landing between the attic and Vader's studio. Neel Suythof needs not to be poking around in here. "He stepped out to get more pigments. He will be back soon." I pick up Tijger and shut the attic door.

"I wished for him to see if he thought I was making progress on my painting," Neel says.

"I am sure you have caught the essence of that straw dummy."

He folds his arms.

"I jest!"

He shakes his head, his tangled hair brushing his shoulders. When he turns to the stairs, I find that I wish he would stay.

"Wait."

He gives me a look of patient annoyance.

"Vader is gone—let us look in his studio. You know how he has been up to something devious lately."

"No, Cornelia! If he wanted us to see whatever is in there—"

I throw open the door. A large canvas, draped by linen, stands in the studio.

The horror in Neel's eyes is too delicious. You would think I was suggesting that we rob a grave.

I skip toward the canvas. "Let us see what is underneath."

"No! He does not want—"

I fling back the drape. The unfinished images of a man leaning toward a woman hover like ghosts against a dead brown background.

Neel speaks in hushed tones as in the presence of God. "Who are they?"

Downstairs, the front door slams.

"Vader!" I flip the drape back over the painting. "Hide!"

"No." Neel turns to face the door. "We poured out our draft, now we must drink it."

I hold my breath as Vader trudges up the wooden stairs. He is not yet to the top when he sees us.

"Mijnheer—" Neel begins.

"So you have found my project. I wondered what was taking you. You children have so little curiosity."

Neel and I exchange glances. Vader had been hiding his work like a hound with a new bone. And he'd been an ogre at breakfast, slamming down his mug and claiming I'd overwatered the ale, which I had. Now he was being sweet?

"You act so surprised." Vader uncovers the canvas. "So, Neel, what do you think of it?"

I close my eyes and pray for Neel to use his best flattery. Keep Vader jolly, so he does not notice his precious family-group painting is missing. Maybe he does know and is toying with me, ready to spring when I least expect it.

"I know not what to think, mijnheer," Neel says. "It is just a beginning."

"Quite right, quite right. I didn't want anyone to see it

before I knew I had it down. I was afraid the image in my head would dry up. But I think I have it now, even though on the canvas it may not look like much."

"May I ask, mijnheer, whom you are portraying?"

Vader smiles. "Not portraits. An allegory."

Neel considers the canvas. "The subject?"

Vader puffs up like a peacock that has wandered over from the New Maze Park. "Tenderest love."

Neel raises his eyebrows.

Vader laughs, then takes a yellow chunk of ochre from its linen wrapping. "I know. An impossible task." He puts the ochre on the hollowed-out grinding slab and begins to pulverize it with a bell-shaped stone pestle. "How do you capture love or hate or any emotion, for that matter? It escapes the painter's brush. We can only hope to simulate how it looks."

Neel nods sadly. "So I have found. Here—let me take that." I cannot help but notice how his forearms bulge as he grinds with the heavy pestle.

"This will be the exception," Vader says, watching him, too. "God is guiding my hand."

Neel does not flinch. He seems not to find Vader the least bit mad. Could he really think God would work through such an imperfect person? "Which biblical story do you use to convey it?" Neel asks as he grinds. "Jesus and his moeder? Anna and Tobit? David"—he glances at me—"and Bathsheba?"

Why does he squirm so when he mentions Bathsheba?

I have no care for the story of the silly woman. Let her have her king David. No difficult choice.

"This time, no story," Vader says. "No Bible, no classics, no writings of the ancients. Just two people, embodying love."

Neel pauses. A blind man could read the doubt on his plain face. "Mijnheer, if anyone could do it, it would be you—but love? It is not like portraying apples in a still life. Love is not an object."

I think of Carel and his pride in painting lemons. "It is better to get a real object right," I say staunchly, "than to be thought mad for painting the impossible."

Vader laughs. "What care I about what people think of me? They've already thought the worst. Anyhow, I am not afraid. I shall trust in God." Vader smiles fondly at the unfinished picture as Neel fetches a jar of linseed oil to work into the ground pigment. "This shall be a present for Titus. To make amends."

A mad picture in exchange for putting a curse on his marriage? Some compensation.

I watch as Vader pours the oil into the pile of yellow powder and Neel mixes it with the edge of a paint knife—a quiet team, working together to make color. Vader has never let me help him.

Anger at them both burns in my belly. Why do they leave me out?

There is a knock on the door.

Glad to get away from the cozy pair, I run down the stairs to answer it.

I open the door to a bright spring morning and Carel the Handsome, bent-kneed under the weight of a rolled-up canvas.

Even as my heart leaps, I gasp and put my hand to my cap. I am a mess.

"The buyer has turned it down," he says. Through my own dismay of being caught in disarray, I notice his golden face is troubled.

The family group? "But it was requested." I can feel my cheeks flame. Now he knows what a failure my vader is, rejected by all, respected by none. I brush desperately at my wrinkled apron.

"I am sorry, Cornelia. It should have sold. I think it is interesting." He shuffles in place. "Where would you like this?"

Vader laughs upstairs. I break out in a sweat.

Carel peers inside. "Is that your vader? Perhaps I should talk to him myself."

"No! No, he is busy. Painting." It is bad enough to be discovered as a slattern by Carel, but to incur Vader's wrath in front of him?

"Put it in there!"

"The kitchen?"

"Yes. It's a good place." I can hide it there until I get a chance to move it.

Carel steps forward with the canvas, then pauses in the entrance hall. He has noticed Vader's picture of Moeder in her shift.

"This way!" I yelp. "Quickly."

I press my hands against my face as he carries the painting through the front room to the kitchen. I am ashamed of the reek of cooked cabbage and the damp, cracked kitchen walls.

"Where should it go?" he asks.

Vader's voice is at the top of the stairs.

"Behind these barrels," I say. "Quickly."

"Cornelia?" Vader calls.

"Surely you have heard about my vader's terrible temper," I whisper. "He will not be happy about this." Not a lie, for certain, though I mean about taking his painting without permission, not his reaction to the buyer's rejecting it. "We must let his choler cool."

No matter the true reason, Carel seems to see the logic in this. He dumps the canvas, then hurries after me through the half door leading into the courtyard outside.

We pause on the step. The van Roop girls are on their side of the courtyard, jumping rope in the crisp April air. "Can you walk?" Carel asks over their singsong verses. The wind whips a shoot of the rose vine that grows near the door, nearly lashing my face. I push it away, scratching my hand on its tiny new thorns.

Inside the house, Vader calls.

"I would like to. Yes."

It is not a walk but a run we break into as we hurry between narrow houses down the alleyway. Several doors away from my own, we burst from the shadows onto the street and are met with the fresh morning sun.

"First warm day of the year," Carel says.

We look before us. Across the canal, the sunlight catches each shiny holly leaf in the hedge of the New Maze Park, turning it into a wall of glittering emeralds. Yellow-green pearls glow on the tips of the linden-tree branches. A frog hops into the canal, sending coins of silver light bobbing on the brown water. The duck family glides past all in a line, save for a duckling who darts at a dragonfly, then races in a panic to catch up with its brothers.

"I'd like to try to paint this scene," Carel says. " 'The Canal Near Cornelia's House on a Sunny Spring Morn.' "

I must not grin like a fool. "Oh, a landscape now? You must have mastered your glass."

He raises his brows. "You remembered? Well, yes. I can now put reflections in reflections. You should see. I am no van Eyck, but I am getting there."

I laugh, then cast a look behind me at my house. I see movement in the window of Vader's studio.

"I would like to paint you," Carel says.

"Me?"

"I know," says Carel, "you must be tired of it. You have probably been painted a hundred times."

"Not really. Sometimes I sit for Neel, but just to hold a position."

We wait for an old man stumping by with his cane to pass. "Your vader has not painted you? He is mad." Carel sees my grimace. "I mean, he is missing an opportunity."

I look doubtful.

"I mean it. If you were my daughter, I would have painted you a thousand times. You are beautiful."

I search for a sign that he is jesting. I have been called many things. Skittish. Willful. A crazy man's daughter.

Never beautiful.

A flock of butterflies has been set free in my stomach. I want to throw back my head and crow. I try to think how my book says I should comport myself, but my brain is full of tumbling puppies. I manage to mumble, "So are you."

His laugh rings out. Two wood doves burst up, their wings whistling, from the linden tree. "You are a different one. No, don't look like that! I mean it well. I am glad you are different."

I can hardly keep from glancing at him as we walk along in silence. Does he realize I am poor? Does he think me awkward and stupid and mad?

As if on cue, the death bells of the Westerkerk sound out. "There are your bells again," I blurt. "Have you tried counting them"—*Lord, can you not stop yourself, girl?*—"since last time?" There. Now I have revealed that I have recalled, one thousand times, every word he last spoke.

He smiles. "They have rung three times a day, on average, though they rang eight times on Thursday and just once on Monday. I have counted the times, hoping we would meet again and I could tell you."

"So you were right. They do ring more these days." I battle

back the silly grin that threatens to swallow my face. He must think me addled, grinning about more deaths.

His face becomes clouded. "I saw a red *P* on a door yesterday," he says quietly, "over on the Kalverstraat."

A tiny pang of fear jabs into my heart. No. I will not be afraid. I will not let it ruin my happiness. "That doesn't mean a great pestilence is afoot. There are always a few isolated cases. People have been keeping the streets cleaner—the city will make bonfires if it gets bad. It's not like it was before."

He nods slowly. "You are right. I am foolish about this sort of thing. It's just that . . ." He looks to me. I wait in encouraging silence. "It's just that I lost my moeder in the last bad year of plague."

I breathe in to dispel the sadness. "In truth, I suffered the same. Five years ago, this July. You aren't being foolish. It still hurts, very much."

"My moeder left us in September. It was horrible." He touches my hand. "I should have known you would understand. We have much in common, don't we?"

I gaze up into his awaiting blue eyes but must look away fast. He will think me a ghoul, grinning like this as we speak of grief.

He stops me beneath a budding linden. He is lifting my chin.

"This is how I will paint you, when you look like this."

My insides are aflame. They push at my very flesh, seeking to burst outside.

I look into his eyes, then at the pink-brown swell of his lips. I nearly swoon as their fullness compacts into a pucker.

"I—"

"Shhhh," he whispers. The gentle pressure of his finger on my lips stuns me into silence.

"How am I to capture you?" His eyes caress me with their warmth. Something inside me strains toward him, frightening me with its insistence.

My throat is so swollen with emotion I can barely swallow. "I should go," I whisper.

I fumble into a turn and run, not feeling the bricks under my feet. Carel Bruyningh touched me. He likes me! Carel Bruyningh. Oh, dear God!

"Cornelia!" he calls after me. "May I see you again?"

I cast a look over my shoulder as he stands beneath the green-sprigged linden, his golden brows raised in hope. It is the best moment in my life.

"Yes!"

Chapter 13

Juno.

Begun about 1661, finished after summer 1665. Canvas.

When I get home, Moeder is not in the kitchen or in the courtyard hanging wash. I hope she is not in the studio, but she is, sitting on a throne, holding a queen's gold rod. She's dressed up in a gold velvet gown that must have cost hundreds. There is no money for St. Nicolaes Day presents, but there is always plenty for things Vader paints in his pictures.

Moeder sees me. She moves to get up.

"Hendrickje, please," Vader says. "You must be still."

"Cornelia is home from school and needs to eat."

"She knows where we keep the cheese," Vader says. "Please, sit. Remember you are Juno, queen of the world, full of wisdom, patience, and goodness."

"I warn you, Rembrandt, I don't feel the least bit patient, good, or wise."

"Hendrickje," Vader says, as if soothing a cat.

"The sampling officials are still waiting and the Trippen have

canceled the rest of their family portraits, you took so long to complete their parents' pictures. Now what are we going to do?"

"They wouldn't have liked them anyway," Vader says. "They want them done in the style of my youth."

"Then why don't you do it? Is it so hard to please people?"

"Even if I try, they find reason to delay payment. I might as well please myself."

"Oh!" Moeder cries, then gets up and leaves. I run after her. She goes into the courtyard, where she jerks the clothes off the line.

"Not now, Cornelia," she says.

I go to the front stoop. Titus finds me there when he lets out Tijger. "What are you doing out here, Bird? It's freezing."

When I don't answer, he sits down next to me. We watch the wood doves peck at something pink on the cobblestones until Tijger springs after them.

"I told Jannetje Zilver I got an ivory doll for St. Nicolaes Day," I say at last.

"That was dumb," Titus says. "Why'd you do that?" Titus knows that I just got some nuts in my shoes, even though the other neighborhood children got apples and soap-bubble pipes and dolls in theirs. Nuts are what I get every year. I wonder what Titus got when he was young.

"She asked me what I got from St. Nicolaes."

"Ohhh."

"I said I would bring the doll to school," I say.

He knocks on my head. "Is your brain as wooden as your clompen?"

"I can never go back to school." I lay my cheek on my knees, facing away from him.

He bounces his fist on my back. "Of course you can, Birdie. We have got things around here that will impress your Jannetje Zilver. Take her one of Vader's helmets."

"Yuck."

"The stupid things are worth a bundle. They're gold plated."

"No."

"Then take in the stuffed bird of paradise."

"I hate that stinky thing! Besides Vader is using it in one of the pictures he's painting now."

"I know—take the arm in the jar."

I scream.

He laughs. "That would fix old Jannetje."

I lay my cheek back on my knee.

He thunks me again. "Worry not, my little Bird. When I am twenty-six, I shall inherit a pile of money from my moeder's family."

"How much?"

"A lot. My moeder's family wasn't poor like . . ."

I look up.

"I'll come and get you," he says, "and we shall be rich as kings."

"Just you and me?"

"Just you and me."

"That doesn't help me now," I say, then turn my cheek to my knee.

He goes back into the house. I stay with my head down and listen to the thumping of my heart. How does it know to keep beating by itself? Could I stop it if I thought about it hard enough? My skin tingles. What if I stopped it and died?

All of a sudden I cannot breathe! I don't know how to make my heart go!

"What is wrong?"

I sit up, startled. The Gold Mustache Man stands next to the porch. I have not seen him for a long while, unless I count the time I thought I saw him last month, when Moeder took me to the picture of the carved-open man. He spoke? He has not done so since I was little.

"Is something wrong?" he asks again.

Who is he? Where does he live? Do Moeder and Vader know him?

"I didn't mean to frighten you." He tips his hat, making the fluffy white feather on it flutter. "Good-bye, my dear."

He is so handsome, so friendly, I don't want him to go.

"I told my friend I had a doll," I say.

He stops, pushes his hat far back on his curly gold hair, and waits.

"A real ivory one." I swallow. "I said I got it from St. Nicolaes."

He smiles. "And I take it you don't have this doll."

I shake my head.

He looks up at the house, then back at me. "Well, some problems have an easy solution." He winks, then puts his finger to his lips in our signal.

I tap my lips back. Is that all he is going to say? Don't go! I shout in my head.

But he turns and walks away, a trim figure in a glossy black cassock.

Why should I have thought he could help? He is just a man who walks by our house sometimes. Simple-head, I scold myself as I go back inside the house. Next you will be hoping the ducks on the canal bring you candy.

Chapter 14

I am in the kitchen slicing a carrot for a stew for the de noen and can think of nothing but Carel. Yesterday he called me beautiful. He is the beautiful one, with his golden curls and pale lashes and skin the color of finest wheat. His straight nose is dusted with nutmeg freckles, and oh, his lips, with the upper slightly fuller than the lower. How can I live without seeing them today?

Neel comes into the kitchen with a mug. "May I have some ale?" he says quietly. He stands before the cask, frowning.

I sweep the carrot from the chopping block and sprinkle it into the pot I have filled with water. "You know you don't have to ask. Help yourself." I go back to my vision of Carel, still smiling at me in the sunlight. His lips, so deep pink-brown and—

Neel pours a draft but does not leave.

"What?" He is ruining my dream.

"I saw you with Bruyningh."

Just hearing the name makes me smile. "Yes. So?"

"Yesterday, by the canal."

"We were walking. Have you an objection?" I rub my hand, my only concession to my desire to hug myself with glee. Neel Suythof's soberness will not frustrate me today.

"Cornelia, I found your vader's painting in the kitchen. Bruyningh brought it back, didn't he?"

I look away.

"I put it in your vader's studio, where it was before you took it."

What does he want from me? "Thank you," I say stiffly. "As the old saying goes, I have been cast in a barrel before a whale and have escaped harm—I am lucky this time."

Vader calls from his studio. "Cornelia?"

I move more quickly than is my custom to the hallway, anxious to get away from Neel and his seriousness. "Yes, Vader?"

"Would you and Neel please come up here?"

"Yes, Vader! He wants us to go up."

"I heard," Neel says.

"What if he has noticed the painting was missing after all? He's crafty like that. Plays as if he doesn't know, then ah-ha, he makes his move."

"Then you shall deal with it," Neel says.

"I don't know how!"

"You can learn."

"Cornelia? Are you coming?" Vader calls.

I trudge up the stairs, glad that Neel is behind me, even though he is in an unusual bad temper.

"What is it?" I ask when we arrive in the studio. I see that the rolled-up canvas of the family group has been neatly placed along one of the cracking walls. Next to it, a breastplate of armor lies on its side, making me think of an empty sea turtle shell.

"I need models for the couple." Vader nods at his unfinished picture. Nearby is Neel's own easel, which Vader has allowed him to set up with the straw dummy before it.

"Us?" I ask.

"I don't know why I didn't think of it sooner," Vader says. "The two of you have got just the right proportions together. Neel, would you mind?"

"I shall be honored, mijnheer."

Vader rubs his hands. "Good. Good. Stand over there. Cornelia, you, too."

I take my place next to Neel. We stand apart.

"Now Neel, take her hand and look in her eyes."

"As in, say, the Arnolfini portrait by van Eyck?"

I roll my eyes. That old thing? I've seen the copy Vader has. The little dog in the painting looks more lively than the newwed couple it portrays. Neel the Serious would think the picture was the image of romantic passion.

"Rather a stiff presentation," Vader says, "but yes. For now."

"Is this necessary?" I say as Neel floats his long-fingered hand in my direction.

"Completely," Vader says.

"Oh, all right." I glare at the rolled-up canvas. If I had known how much trouble that foolish picture would cause me, I would have never taken it.

Neel closes his hand around mine. It's surprising how warm it is, and large. My own hand feels quite small, protected, almost, within his.

"You children are going to have to look at each other," Vader says. "My subject is love, not revulsion."

I do as ordered, but I do not have to look happy.

The faintest pained smile appears at the corners of Neel's plain lips.

Vader begins dabbing the canvas with his brush. I want to wiggle my hand, to look away.

"Mijnheer," Neel says to Vader but still facing me. "May I speak?"

"Certainly. I'm not working on the heads today."

"Then why must we gape at each other like two lovesick doves!" I exclaim.

"Positioning," Vader says.

I let my hand go limp and give Neel a look that assures him that I would rather be emptying chamber pots than continuing to contemplate his serious countenance.

Neel holds my hand, unperturbed. "Mijnheer, I am thinking of putting aside the picture on which I am working to pursue a Prodigal Son."

"A subject I once explored with great relish." Vader adds a

stroke to his canvas. "I had a wonderful time painting that picture, though Saskia did not entirely approve of the project. She objected to dressing up like a whore, though she got her fringe benefit. That painting resulted in our first Cornelia."

"Vader! How can you speak like thus before Neel and me?"

"What?"

"What you just said!"

"Child, must you always have such a burr up your arse?" Vader rests his leg on his stool and sighs. "Saskia. What a delight she was."

I am so mortified before Neel that my next thought pops out unbidden. "You loved her more than my mother." I glance at Neel, my face reddening.

Vader has the nerve to act surprised. "Why would you say such a thing?"

I try to pull away from Neel, furious with myself for revealing too much in front of him, but Neel won't let me go.

"What indication did I ever give that I favored one over the other?" Vader says. "They were entirely different. I loved them both."

"Never mind," I mutter.

"I have found," Vader says, "that it is possible to love more than one person with all your heart. I might even admit that it is possible to love more than one at the same time." He sighs. "This lesson comes not easily."

Neel be damned. "You could have made her happy," I say. "But you didn't."

"How do you mean? I cherished the woman."

I glance at Neel, then whisper harshly, "Then why didn't you marry her?"

Assurance bleeds from Vader's face, leaving behind a weary old man. "I wanted to, Cornelia."

"What stopped you?"

Vader opens his mouth, then shuts it again. His face is as gray as the walls.

Neel squeezes my hand. "Mijnheer, about this Prodigal Son painting I wish to pursue . . ."

Vader looks at him as if he'd forgotten he was in the room.

"I am not sure how to stage it," Neel says.

"Just take your time with it," Vader murmurs.

"I am interested in forgiveness, in its healing powers."

"What?"

"The healing powers of forgiveness."

Vader's smile comes in slow degrees, like a man swimming from the depths of the ocean to the surface. "And you wish to portray this in paint?"

"Yes, mijnheer."

"Good boy."

"How long will this take?" I exclaim.

"Take?" Vader says.

"This standing here for your picture!"

"Months," Vader says.

"Months? I cannot bear it!"

"You cannot bear what, Worry Bird?" It is Titus, in the

doorway, looking dashing in a new black satin doublet. I jerk free of Neel and run to him.

"What a greeting!" Titus pulls back from my hug.

"You never come."

"Well," he says, brushing off his sleeves, "soon you shall have me for hours on end. I'm here to ask you to dinner on Sunday. You, too, Neel, if you'd like." He smiles brightly, as if the invitation weren't really an afterthought.

"Thank you," Neel says, "but I think I am engaged."

"Too bad. Vader? How does dinner Sunday sound? We're having calf's foot and tripe with green peas, a roast beef with butter and cheese, and all the trimmings."

"Bringing out the fatted calf," Vader says.

"What?"

He winks at Neel. "Nothing. Nothing."

"We have a new cook. Cornelia, you will have to tell me what you think of him."

Titus knows that my experience with food has been mostly limited to cabbage soup, bread, and cheese, but I am willing to play along with him. "We'll see." Carel must know about fine food, coming from a wealthy family as he does. I must learn my way around it.

"So how much did you get for your picture, Vader?" Titus asks.

"What picture?"

"The family group," Titus says.

"I told you, I wasn't selling it."

Titus squints at me.

"He said he couldn't sell it," I say pointedly. "Remember?"

"What's going on here?" Vader says. "I saw that youngster who works for van Uylenburgh prowling around here yesterday, but I thought he was just keen on Cornelia—girl as pretty as her, suitors are bound to come sniffing about. Is there more to the story than that?"

Vader called me pretty? "No, Vader," I say. "We just took a walk, that is all."

"What does he want?" Vader says. "Who put him up to it?"

Neel watches me intently.

"No one, Vader!"

Neel clears his throat. "Excuse me, Titus, but I think perhaps I might be available Sunday for dinner after all. Is the offer still good?"

Titus shrugs. "Certainly, Neel, come on if you will. I've got a new cook from Leuven," he says. "He claims to know both French and Flemish cookery. He did not come cheaply, I shall tell you that. Do you know the price of cooks these days?"

Neel listens soberly as Titus carries on about the expense of being the master of the House of the Gilded Scales, but not before he has cast a questioning glance at me. I rub my hand. I can still feel the warm strength of his fingers. And Vader said we would be modeling for months.

Well, I have no choice in the matter but to suffer with Neel.

Chapter 15

Saskia as Flora.

Ca. 1634. Canvas.

I have just awoken and am scratching my fingernail through the frost furring the window when Moeder calls from the kitchen.

"Neeltje! Please go out and get the milk."

I pad through the front room and entrance hall and tug open the heavy wooden door. I have started toward the milk the dairyman has left on our stoop in a tin can when I see something propped against the step.

I crouch down. A breeze plucks at the locks of real brown hair glued to the head of an ivory-faced doll.

I snatch her up, hug her to me, then hold her out again, her red velvet skirt flowing. She is mine. She's got to be mine. She was left on my stoop.

I put a careful finger to her cold lips, curved in a pink painted smile, then lift her skirt. A real petticoat—two of them! I rock her with joy. She is far prettier than Jannetje Zilver's old doll, her skirt and bodice fancier, her hair thicker. I will name her a special name, a lady's name. Saskia.

No. Not her. I don't like her or her ugly picture on the wall. I don't care if she was Titus's moeder.

I feel something stiff on the doll's back. I turn her around and lift the little card tied around her waist.

"From St. Nicolaes."

Chapter 16

Book in hand, I lean out the front window and drink in the sweet melancholy sounds of morning: the willow leaves murmuring in sleepy protest at a breeze, the wooden groan of the windmill turning at the end of the street, a solitary dove cooing. A male duck wings from somewhere in the park to the canal with a frenzied quack, then splashes softly onto the water next to the moeder duck, whose five ducklings dart forward on webbed tiptoes to join them. Into this calm, ring the bells of the Westerkerk, not the solemn *bong* of the death bell, but the happy peal of the smaller ones, calling the faithful to worship. It is the morning of the Sunday Vader and I are to dine with Titus, and we are not going to church like the rest of Amsterdam. No church will have us.

I wonder if Carel is at church now. Other, prettier girls could be trying to catch his eye as they sit next to their wealthy vaders. And he could be gazing back at them, his mind far from the unkempt daughter of a failed doodler. He could be smiling at one right now, his blue eyes bright, his straight teeth shining . . .

I throw down my book. Rules of comportment indeed! What was I thinking? No amount of handkerchief fluttering or curtsey dropping on my part is enough to win a boy like Carel. I could perform with all the comportment in the world and still not compete with a rich merchant's pretty daughter. He had said he liked me. But why would he? Capturing the heart of a poor man's daughter was just a sport to him, and I had let him touch me! Now I shall probably never see him again. It has been two days since we talked and I fear he shall come no more.

Up in his studio, the man who ruins my chances with Carel has his table pulled next to the open window. A moist wind pours in as I peer over his shoulder, where he sketches an older man placing his hands on the back of a kneeling younger one as in a blessing.

Bitterness seeps into my gut like poison. "Don't you think God frowns on you," I say, "working on a Sabbath?"

Vader's goose quill pen scratches on the vellum as he works. "I believe by now He already knows I am an impossible old rapscallion."

Ja, that is for certain.

"Yet still, He gives me gifts. Why, I do not know. His generosity perplexes me. But if He is going to give me gifts, I am going to use them. I suspect to do otherwise would displease Him. So to answer your question, no, I don't think God is angry about my working now." Vader stops sketching. "Thinking about it, this *is* my form of worship." He sees my frown. "What do you want?"

In truth, I am not sure why I had wandered upstairs—to make him as miserable as I am? There is no Neel to provide a buffer between us—Neel won't be coming to work on a Sabbath. As boring as he is, at least Neel is company. I see two mugs and several empty plates scattered around the studio. "I came to clean up your mess."

"A tidy girl, just like your mother." He dips his pen into his inkpot, then draws again.

"That is true. I am not very much like you." I am as thrilled by my boldness as by the possibility that my statement might be true.

He stops to watch me gather the dishes into my apron, his flabby face buckled in a frown. "No, you wouldn't be."

I cannot hear over the clatter of plates as I shift my apron. "What?"

He sucks in a breath as if to speak, then shakes his head and goes back to his sketching.

I study his drawing as I pick up a mug from his table. "You ought to turn the man's head to the side when he kneels before the other man. Straight on, he looks to be butting the standing man with his head."

Vader considers my suggestion, then with a few strokes of

brown ink, turns the kneeling man's head. He regards the change. "Good eye. Thank you."

I squelch the pride that rises within me.

"What's this scene supposed to be?" I ask gruffly.

"Guess," he says with an impish grin.

Not this old game again. But I study the two men, the young one seemingly begging for forgiveness, the older one granting it.

I shift the dishes in my apron. With great casualness, I say, "The Prodigal Son?"

"You are good."

I force the smile from my lips. One good guess does not a genius make. "It's just that Neel had mentioned it, that's all."

He gazes at me as if looking through my skin to my hidden inner self. "Since you seem to be full of opinions, are there any other suggestions you might have?"

In my almost fourteen years of life, he has never asked me such a thing. Furious at my insides for their traitorous fluttering, I peer at the picture as if his eyes were not on me. I rattle my dishes and think.

"Isn't the returning son supposed to be broken down and penniless? You have him wearing sandals. How could he afford them?"

Vader puts his finger to his lip and examines the drawing. From within the maze across the canal, a peacock squawks. At last he says, "Good point."

"Anyone could see that," I mumble.

I will not grin.

He returns to the sketch. His hand that holds the pen is spotted with age as he works on the son's feet. "Poor Titus did not have the gift," he says.

I dare not breathe. Go on, old man.

He adds a brown dash to the vader's robe. "I worked with the lad from the cradle. I taught him perspective, coloration, style, everything; then with all this knowledge, when he was your age, he produced his first painting. Do you know what it was?"

I shake my head quickly.

"A dog. Which would be very fine and good, except that it looked like a sheep. A surprised sheep, at that. Poor lad. He worked on it for months, and I worked with him some more, yet still—a shocked sheep."

As he continues his sketching, I stare at the strands of gray hair that span the bare crest of his skull. Teach me how to draw. Teach me perspective. Teach me how to make color, how to blend paint dabs on a palette. Teach me it all.

"I need to prevail on you for your skills," he says, not looking up.

My heart leaps. After all these years. He has seen my merit and is going to teach me. *Breathe in, calmly now.* "Yes?"

"I need you to shave me for dinner at Titus's today."

My hope collapses like a burnt sod of peat. "Shave you?"

I should have known better. Had I not learned long ago that disappointment is the coin he deals me? How could

I forget running into the house with my newfound ivory-faced doll, thanking Vader over and over for giving her to me for St. Nicolaes Day after all, and such a doll at that! At first Vader had acted surprised to see her, then glad, then he promptly gave her to Moeder, who was made to trade her for bread at the baker's. He said somebody's mistake for putting her on our stoop was our gain. "Manna from heaven," he had said with a laugh.

Now he turns around to look at me. "Is something wrong?"

"No. Nothing."

"Just a moment and you can shave me."

I am too defeated to argue.

Soon I had dumped the dishes in the kitchen and we are at the back of the house, where I lather his furry cheeks with soap and brush, my mood as rotten as a wasp-eaten apple. You would think that he who entrusts a girl with a razor to his throat ought to take more care to humor her.

Vader's face sufficiently lathered, I sharpen the razor on the strop like I have seen Titus do, only more slowly, carefully drawing the blade along the leather strap away from my body, then dragging it cautiously toward me. But as frightening as it is to strop a razor, the shaving scares me doubly. Much as I'd like to see the old rogue gone, I don't wish to dispatch him from this world with a cut. I hesitate over him, trembling, with the gleaming five-inch blade.

He looks up from his bed with the innocence of a child, his hands folded neatly over his belly. "I suggest this time that you pull my skin as you go. You have to stretch out this old rooster wattle if you're not going to nick it."

I don't want to touch the old fowl, but I don't wish to have Magdalena think poorly of us when he appears at her table with a fresh set of cross-hatchings. Gingerly, I lay two fingers against his soapy jaw, and holding down the loose skin, slowly mow a path though the lather, resulting in a strip of elderly skin as smooth as a baby's rump.

"Go on," he says.

Three more times I draw down the blade as he lies as still as a child getting picked over by his moeder for nits. Three more times I have not cut him. I swish the blade in the bowl of water, proud that I've done no damage so far.

"Leave the mustache," he says.

I gaze at where the left edge of his mustache once was.

"Did you get it?" he asks.

I nod.

He frowns, then waves his hand. "Oh well, then take the rest of it. I shall start a new fashion. It was getting in my broth, regardless."

I scowl at his childishly red lips sticking out from the lather. I must touch them if I'm not to cut him.

He looks up at me. "I am not going to bite, you know."

"Oh, all right," I say. I yank down his top lip as he rolls his eyes comically. I suppress a laugh as I draw down the razor. As a bank of bristles embedded in soapsuds rolls before the razor like dirty snow before a shovel, another mustache suddenly comes to mind. A gold one, shining in the sun. I think of the gold-mustache man who used to stop in front of the house and give me our little sign. It has been years since I have seen him—since the plague that took Moeder. In my melancholy that followed her death, I forgot to look for him, until at last, I forgot to think of him at all. I wonder what had become of him. Had he been taken by the contagion, too?

Vader flinches. "Ouch!"

Blood wells up from a nick just above his lip.

"Oh! Sorry!" Quickly, I dab at it with my apron.

"No matter, no matter." Vader pushes away my apron, then staunches the flow with the sleeve of his shirt. When at last no more blood spots his sleeve, he settles back on the bed. "Keep going, keep going. You were doing well."

He closes his eyes as if confident I won't butcher him.

When I have finished, he sits up and pulls the dingy linen cloth from around his neck to admire himself in a hand mirror.

"Excellent, if I may say so," he says. "You've got very good control of your hands."

"I do?"

"You know you do. You have a delicate touch—that's important for a painter."

I duck my head as I rinse the razor, not wanting to show how much I value these words. I must change the subject before I give myself away.

I throw the sudsy water out the window. "Do you remember," I say lightly, "having a friend that had a bright gold mustache and golden curls—a younger man, good-looking, I suppose some would say."

He lowers the mirror.

"A friend of yours," I continue, "with bright gold hair. He used to come by here a lot. Do you remember someone like that?"

"I don't know what you're saying," he says sharply.

Something inside me turns over in pain. Why does he act this way, when we were just beginning to speak with each other? "It is nothing."

I walk stiffly from the room and wait in the kitchen, my stomach sour, until Neel arrives. Later, when the three of us walk to the House of the Gilded Scales for de noen, I keep my distance from Vader. He will not look at me, either. Neel gazes between us, his somber face wrinkled with puzzlement; then he speaks to Vader of a painting by van der Helst he has just seen at the Stock Exchange.

Easily drawn into criticizing another artist's painting, Vader takes up the conversation and thinks no more of me.

Chapter 17

At table, that afternoon of our first dinner at the House of the Gilded Scales, Magdalena delicately stretches her creamy neck in my direction. Below finely haired brows, she blinks pale almond-shaped eyes like a dainty creature unused to strong light. "Cornelia, sister, is the beef cooked to your liking?"

Except at Jannetje Zilver's house, I have had beef twice before in my life. Once was at kermis, the town festival in the fall, when they roasted an ox in the square by the poultry market and everyone got too drunk to chase me off. The other was at the wedding feast of neighbors who were Moeder's friends until Vader got in an argument with them over the noise they made cutting stone in their courtyard, though cutting stone is what the man did for his living. Ruined his concentration, Vader said. Magdalena's beef is good as far as I can tell. But it is hard to delight in the eating of it, after Vader has turned on me for no reason and the thought of Carel flirting with girls at church has burned a hole in my stomach. "Yes," I say. "It's good."

"What's wrong, Cornelia?" Titus says, "You've been unnaturally quiet."

Even if I had not been unsettled by Vader and by jealous thoughts of Carel, I would not know what to say at a table set with blue-and-white china, ruby glass goblets, and a silver saltcellar shaped like a swan. I am used to our battered table in the kitchen.

Fortunately, Magdalena does not wait for my answer. "Last week," she addresses the table in general, "we entertained Silvius Lam, the world's leading expert on mosses. He has been all around the world, examining the different mosses."

"Is that so," Vader says, his mouth full.

"He said there are some excellent mosses in America," Titus says. "According to Mijnheer Lam, it is a particularly mossy continent."

"He thought our cook quite good," Magdalena says. "Excellent with organ meat."

"Our cook is not cheap," Titus says.

"I like the beef," I say.

Magdalena bestows her dimples upon me. "The recipe is from Johanna de Geer."

"Magdalena is in a church group with Hendrik Trip's wife, Johanna," Titus says proudly. "They visit orphanages and give them old clothes. Magdalena and Johanna are quite good friends, you know."

Magdalena lowers her face modestly. "We do a few simple works of charity together. As Johanna says, it is a woman's duty to help the poor."

I nod as daintily as possible as Vader continues tucking into his food. In my book on comportment, I have read that charity is one of the prettier virtues for a woman to develop. And Johanna de Geer could well afford to be charmingly charitable. She is one of the richest women in Amsterdam.

Magdalena looks up, her pretty mouth opening as if she cannot believe the brilliant idea that has just struck her. "Cornelia," she says, "I'm thinking of going to my cloth merchant on Tuesday. Johanna has told me he has received a new shipment of silks from the Orient. Would you be interested in accompanying me? Perhaps I might find you material for a new frock." She can barely contain her radiant smile, thrilled with the prospect of being so charitable.

"Oh, no! I couldn't ask you to do that." I cannot go to the cloth merchant's establishment in my old-fashioned lace collar and worn brown dress. I will be as a fish out of the sea in a place in which Johanna de Geer shops

"Sure you could," Titus says. "Excellent idea, Magdalena. No arguments, Bird."

I glance at Vader but he appears not to be listening. Neel keeps his gaze on his plate. He has been eating so quietly at the far end of the table, I have nearly forgotten he was there. Beneath her silver-blond crown of ringlets and braids, Magdalena waits for an answer, her pretty face all sweet concern and generosity. I have no choice.

"Thank you," I say.

"Sister," Magdalena insists.

The words feel awkward on my lips. "Thank you, sister."

"I shall call on you at nine o'clock, then. Would that suit?"

"Yes." I remember my manners. "Please. Sister. Unless—Vader, do I have to model?" Even being captive to Vader and Neel would be preferable to exposing myself to certain shame.

"Go." Vader wipes his mouth with his napkin. "I can work on the other figure in my painting, if Neel would be so good as to remain."

Neel speaks up for the first time since we sat down to dinner. "Of course, mijnheer."

"Why don't you just spring for some models, Vader?" Titus says. "Surely there are some beggars in the neighborhood who could use some coin."

"Neel and Cornelia are perfect," Vader says.

Ha. Titus knows the reason Vader does not hire models these days. No stuivers.

Just then a gray cat leaps onto the open window. Magdalena screams.

"Titus! Remove that beast, quickly!"

With a screech of chair legs on tile, Titus gets up from the table and shoos away the cat with his napkin.

"They harbor the distemper," Magdalena says, patting her breast. "Johanna de Geer has heard the cases of contagion are growing again. Cornelia, do you still keep that cat of yours?"

"Tijger?" I think of Carel's increasing count of the death

bells. He'd said he'd seen a house marked with a *P* on the Kalverstraat. How many cases will there be before the contagion tips into a full-blown plague? A tingle slithers up my spine.

"You must get rid of it immediately!" Magdalena cries. "It is a danger to all of our health."

"We had him during the last contagion," I say.

"And wasn't there a death?" she demands.

Titus puts his hand on hers. "Now, sweetest, we survived, didn't we?" he says lightly, but his words cannot take away the memory she has evoked. We eat in strained silence, spoons clicking on china, as the specter of the pestilence with its plague wardens banging on doors, its acrid smell of fires to burn the possessions of the dead, its wagons trundling by, arms and legs flopping over the sides, floats above us.

A mechanical clock chimes its golden tune on the sideboard. "Vader," Titus says, "what did you say you were working on?"

Vader swallows his mouthful. "It's a surprise."

The rest at table breathe a silent sigh for a change in subject.

"Being mysterious, are you?" Titus says with a grin.

Magdalena lifts her head as if being brave, then offers her tiny pearl teeth in a smile. "Vader, can you at least say where you got the idea?"

Vader stabs a chunk of meat with his knife and puts it in his mouth. "God."

Magdalena raises her slivers of brows.

"I think what she means, Vader," Titus says, "is did you see something that inspired you? What was it in your daily life that set off the spark?"

Vader swallows his mouthful. "I cannot claim any such credit. It was all His idea."

Like not attending church. How convenient to do whatever one wishes, then to claim God has made one do it.

Titus wipes his hands on his gold brocade napkin. "Vader—"

"It took me a while to learn to sit back and let Him do what He wishes, but I am finally getting the hang of it." Vader smiles. "I used to think I was the great one, that I alone was the genius. Rembrandt van Rijn, the miller's son—boy wonder! Ruben's heir! Leonardo of the North! I know better now. I don't know why God chose me, but I will shut up and listen, if that is what He wants."

The room is quiet except for Vader's renewed chewing of food. What troubles me is that I want to believe him.

I am glad when Magdalena speaks up. "What are you working on, Neel?" she asks brightly.

He clears his throat. "A Prodigal Son, actually."

"Haven't Prodigal Sons been done rather much?" Titus says. "The one Vader did with my . . ." He frowns, his spoon poised at his mouth. "Well, I hope you will at least have the good sense to use models from the neighborhood if you have to paint sinners."

I flash a nervous glance at Magdalena. Does she know that Vader once painted Titus's mother—her cousin—as a whore?

He portrayed our dear Saskia in the act of being dandled on his lap, painting his own grinning self as the bad son before he'd turned good.

"I don't know," says Vader. "It brings so much more depth to a painting when you use people you know."

"Yes," Titus says pointedly, "but what if those people take offense about the roles in which they are depicted?"

I frown at Neel, who has stopped eating to watch me. I wonder if he would feel as loyal to Vader if he knew Vader was working on his own new Prodigal Son.

"You shouldn't complain," Vader says. "I have painted you as an angel speaking to St. Matthew and as a monk."

Titus laughs. "Appropriately enough. But others not painted as favorably could be hurt."

Even with Neel's gaze upon me, my memory crawls on its own to a place I don't wish it to go. I see a red ribbon winding down . . .

Neel speaks up. "My Prodigal Son will be different, at least from any I have seen. I wish to take up the story at a further point in the telling, when the vader is forgiving the son, not when the son is in his debauchery. My aim is to show the vader's forgiveness. How sweet it is to him."

"Good luck," says Titus.

Vader sees me watching him. "Neel and I have been talking," he says to me, responding to my unspoken accusation of stealing Neel's idea. So this is what he had been sketching this morning.

Jealousy flames up within. Vader can work with Neel on a

painting but not me. They are in their own snug little world, better artists than me, better than Carel, better than everyone.

"Why don't you do still lifes?" I exclaim to Neel. "They are pretty, they fetch a good price, and everyone likes them. What's so wrong with painting lemons?"

"Nothing," Neel says, "but that is not what I'm called to do."

I scowl at his serious face. He's as bad as Vader. They deserve each other. Let them paint together in Vader's cramped and dreary workshop while Carel becomes famous and even richer for his lemons. And I—I shall be a virtuous lady, handing out linen shifts to hungry orphans, and my husband, if not Carel, will be someone like him.

But, oh dear Lord, if only it could be Carel.

Chapter 18

Bathsheba with King David's Letter.

1654. Canvas.

My front tooth is loose—a top one. For days I have pushed it with my tongue, checking to see if it could be tightened back up. It hasn't. Now it hangs by a bony thread, as if something inside won't let go of it.

I go find Moeder, scrubbing the stairs.

"Not now, Cornelia." She pulls a dripping gray rag from her bucket. "Frederik Rihel is coming. It's an important commission." She wrings water from her rag and slaps it on a stair.

Jannetje Zilver lost her front teeth last year. Something must be terribly wrong with mine since they have not dropped out. What if there are no new ones to come in behind them? If the tooth goes and there is no new one I will be ugly. Moeder will never call me pretty puss anymore. Vader will never paint me like he does Titus.

I feel a crunch in my mouth and taste blood on my tongue. The hair prickles on my neck as I fold back my lip and pick out a jagged bit of pearl. My tooth.

"Neeltje!" Moeder sits back on her heels. "Look at your cat!"

At the top of the wet stairs, Tijger is giving himself a bath.

"He will track up my stairs," she says. "What are you waiting for? Please get him right now."

Moeder's voice is more cross than usual. Now is not the time to break the news that her puss is permanently ugly. I take four giant steps up the stairs in my stocking feet and grab Tijger.

"Where am I to put him?" I call down. My stomach aches with worry about my tooth.

"Anywhere!" she cries. "In the attic for now!"

I look at the door on the other side of the landing and draw in a breath. I don't like it in there.

Clutching Tijger close, I open the attic door and walk slowly into the room. The only light comes through a small, round, dusty window. An empty birdcage hangs from the rafters. It smells like tar and dust and old bones. I want to cry.

Something skitters across the floor.

I jump back. Tijger springs from my arms so fast I am knocked into something wall-like behind me. A heavy cloth slumps on top on me. I scream and struggle out from under it, then come face-to-face with a towering canvas.

It is a painting—Vader's work. I recognize his colors. Brown and yellow and red. In the center of it, a lady sits on a cloth. She is big, bigger than real size.

Other than a velvet necklace and a band around her arm, she is naked.

I have never seen a lady's naked form before. Only bad women show their bodies—being naked is a sin. Even Moeder gets but half-undressed when she washes. I stare at the bare lady's body, at the dark V between the legs; I memorize the breasts. Then I follow the red ribbon winding up her neck like a snake. In her hair, there is a string of red beads. I come to the face. It is turned to the side.

My insides drop.

No. Not her. No, God.

"Neeltje," says Moeder.

I jump.

She stands in the doorway. "What are you doing?"

The quiet floats like dust between us as she follows my eyes to the picture. When the deep bong of the death bells breaks the silence, Moeder turns her head to listen.

The look on her face is as in the picture.

My inside self pushes at my throat like it wants to get out. I'm going to be sick.

"It is all right, Cornelia," she says.

She is worse than Vader. He is mean and shouts but doesn't hide that he is bad. Moeder acts good, but she is not. She is not who I thought she was.

"Cornelia?"

I push past her.

She doesn't call after me.

Chapter 19

The silvery loops of Magdalena's shining braids and ringlets bounce lightly as she threads her way across the cobblestones of Dam Square. As it is surprisingly warm this the sixth day of April, she wears no cape, just a lilac velvet gown with the skirt drawn up to show the intricate design of the silver brocade skirt below. With her gauzy white linen collar wrapped around her shoulders like folded wings, and the single ostrich feather she holds like a fluffy wand, she looks every inch the Fairy Queen. Meanwhile all around us dogs bark, peddlers call, and lepers shake their rattles. Magdalena is a pearl among swine, even when trailed by a tattered brown shadow. Me.

A team of horses clops heavily by, straining at their harnesses to pull a wagon heaped with barrels. Magdalena taps her hand with her ostrich feather, pausing for me to catch up. "We haven't far to go to Mijnheer Brower's shop. Are you tired?"

My shoes pinch so badly that I can barely walk. They are Moeder's and too small, but my own pair is too shoddy to be worn in public. "I am fine, thank you."

"Sister."

"Thank you, sister."

She smiles. "You are going to love Mijnheer Brower's. His cloth is peerless. All imported. Straight from the Orient, and of the highest quality, too. All the Trippen buy their cloth there. Johanna swears by it. Maybe we shall see her there."

My stomach rolls.

"The marvelous thing about Mijnheer Brower," Magdalena says, raising her voice above a ratcatcher's loud boasts of his wares, "is that he takes markdowns at the drop of a bonnet. I simply say, 'Oh, mijnheer, this material smells like Chinamen!' or 'Mijnheer, are you *sure* this was not soiled upon by your dog?' and down he'll mark it. I get the best quality at a fraction of the price. You should never pay full price on anything, you know. Why put your gold in someone else's pockets?"

There's a man over by the corner of the Town Hall. Though his face is hidden by the shadow of his hat, he appears to be staring at us through the crowd. Magdalena's beauty must be attracting him. She is probably used to such attention.

"Those are pretty beads," Magdalena says, pointing at me with her feather. "Coral, are they?"

"I think so. I don't know." I touch the strand around my neck. I had taken them out from under my pillow, where they'd been hiding for years, and had thrown them on this morning at the last minute, after I had looked in the mirror and seen the pale brown ghost standing before it. I needed something to brighten me up, and the necklace was the only good piece I had.

"Coral is sweet," Magdalena says. "I had several stones set in a collar for my dog. The brown and white of his ears are so pretty against the red." She blinks as she smiles, indicating that only a hound would be caught dead wearing the stones.

The man by the Town Hall has left his post and is picking his way through the crowd. He's moving in our direction. Does he know Magdalena?

"I prefer pearl," Magdalena says. "Titus gave me these for our wedding." She pushes back a mass of shiny ringlets with her feather. "Are they not pretty?"

I pull my gaze from the man to look at the pearl drop, large as a chestnut, dangling from her thin earlobe. How nice for Titus to have wed so well. A few months ago he couldn't even afford bread.

Magdalena lifts her chin and smiles. "Do you know this man?" she says out of the side of her dainty mouth.

The man from the Town Hall steps in our path. He holds his thick but upright frame, suited in fine black wool, in the easy way of a man used to being admired. A friendly grin creases the coarse red flesh of his clean-shaven lower face—his skin has the look of someone fond of his ale, or perhaps too long at sea. Still, there is something boyishly handsome about the jaw visible beneath the wide brim of his hat. Even without seeing his eyes, I can tell he's a man's man, and a woman's man, and he knows it.

"Good day, mevrouw." He sweeps low in a bow to Magdalena and removes his hat, revealing stray filaments of gold in his graying mass of curls, then replaces it before I can take measure of his face. "I hope I have not alarmed you. I am an old friend of your husband." He takes her hand. "Nicolaes Bruyningh."

I stifle a gasp. Carel's uncle.

He does not notice me. "Congratulations on your marriage," he says to Magdalena. "I saw you and Titus at the jeweler's shop several weeks back, when I was at the goldsmith's next door, but did not want to disturb you, especially if Titus was on the brink of making a purchase you greatly desired." He smiles, then kisses her hand. "It is good to make your acquaintance at last."

Magdalena laughs. Her cheeks are tinged with the palest pink as she flutters her feather. "The pleasure is mine."

He turns to me. "And this is—?"

I strain to see into the shadows of his hat. There is something quite familiar about him.

"This is my sister-in-law," Magdalena says, "Cornelia."

He takes my hand in his own, which is surprisingly dry and hard, as if his insides have solidified into stone. "So this is the famous Cornelia. I have heard about you from my nephew Carel."

"You have?"

Magdalena laughs fondly at my clumsy response, as one would at a trained monkey.

"Oh yes," says Nicolaes Bruyningh. "All good things, I assure you. He says you have an eye for art. You must get that from your vader."

I glow from within. Carel spoke of my talent? "Yes, mijnheer."

"You and he must be very close."

Does he mean my vader or Carel? I try harder to see under his hat to determine whom he might mean, but he pulls back.

He eases the brim of his hat down farther over his face. "It is good," he says suavely, "to keep family ties."

I know enough from reading *Maidenly Virtues* to nod politely, though I have no idea what he is trying to say.

"With my brother living next door, I have been able to watch Carel and his brothers and sisters grow up right under my nose," he says. "I heard them cry when they were hungry, laugh when they were playing, whimper when they were sick. It was almost like raising them myself—without the sleepless nights, of course. Carel is the baby of the family, you know."

I strive for the tone of a merchant's well-bred daughter. "He speaks most admiringly of his older brothers and sisters, mijnheer."

"Yes, well, perhaps I should have you and Carel around for

dinner sometime," he says. "An old bachelor like me could use some lively company at table."

"Oh," Magdalena says, "that would be most kind, would it not, Cornelia? Titus and I just had her dine with us ourselves. She is a complete delight."

"I imagine she is. My nephew was not born a fool. Well, I must not detain you ladies from your business." Nicolaes Bruyningh bows. "Good day."

"Imagine that," Magdalena says as soon as we have walked a sufficient distance away from him. "Young Carel is speaking of you. When he gets a little older, he will be quite the catch, you know. The Bruyninghs are wonderfully wealthy. All those ships."

I shiver with excitement as I picture myself dressed in glossy silks and drinking a cup of chocolate in a stately mansion. But such joys would not be half the pleasure of just being the wife of Carel Bruyningh, and having his iris-blue gaze upon me each morning . . . and each night. My knees buckle with momentary weakness.

"I tell you who you must watch out for," says Magdalena as we continue across the square, "is that apprentice boy your vader keeps, Ned, Will . . ."

"Neel?" I look over my shoulder. Nicolaes Bruyningh stands where we left him, though housewives and carts and groups of men cross before him. When he sees me looking, he tips his hat. I turn back around, blushing. I have seen him before. I know I have.

"I suppose that is his name," says Magdalena. "The boy

who came to dinner on Sunday. Rather a serious young thing. Anyhow, do you know if he has money?"

"Neel? I don't know. Enough to pay my vader. Why?"

"Because the boy is obviously smitten with you."

"Neel?" We round the corner onto a narrow street lined with neatly kept step-gabled houses. I laugh even though my feet are threatening mutiny in my moeder's shoes.

"Oh, yes, my dear, your Neel. He could not keep his eyes off you."

"If that's true, it would be only because he had no other place to look."

"Sister," she scolds, "you know that's not true."

It appears she is not jesting with me. "Neel could not care about me in a romantic way. I have given him no reason whatsoever to have such feelings."

Now it is Magdalena's turn to laugh. "Dear sister, since when has that stopped a boy from falling in love with a girl?"

Just then, her little fingers dig into my arm.

"What is it?" I ask.

She stabs her feather at a blue-shuttered house just ahead. The blue of its door has been slashed with a red-painted *P*.

She tugs me back in the direction in which we came. "I had hoped the contagion would visit only the poor this time. The rest of us now know well enough to keep clean and free of bad vapors. But this is a good street—I have a wine merchant down here. These persons should know better."

Like a corpse in a canal, a red-painted *P* floats to the surface of my memory. I remember hands upon my arms, pulling me back. I hear a little girl crying . . .

"Fortunately," Magdalena says, "I know a different way to Mijnheer Brower's establishment." I hurry after her on pained feet as she retreats to the Dam, then sails down another side street. We dash this way and that down several passageways, arriving at last at a snug brick shopfront.

"Here we are!" she says.

I enter the store, newly aware of my shoddy brown dress as a stout man with a thin smile comes around the counter to greet us.

"Magdalena Jansdochter!" he cries, using Magdalena's familiar name.

He takes her hand and bows, exposing the gray wisps of hair that escape like smoke from his shiny pate, while equally as cozily, she coos, "Jan Pieterszoon! Johanna says you have some wonderful new stock. My sister-in-law and I wish to look at it."

As if appraising a milk cow at sale, he surveys my shoes, gown, and collar, pausing a moment on my beads. His blink tells me he would not collar even a dog with such lowly stones.

"Oh, look at this brocade!" Magdalena has seized a bolt of the richest turquoise and gold. "Jan Pieterszoon, this is heavenly. Where is it from?"

"India." Mijnheer Brower abandons his scrutiny of me to rush to her side. He brings out bolts of velvets and silks and lengths of shimmering satins. Magdalena exclaims over each as I keep watch on the door, praying no fine customers will come.

The clock in the church outside has rung after two rotations and my feet have settled into a low roar of pain when at last Magdalena returns to the brocade that had caught her eye when we first arrived. She lowers her small nose to the heavy bolt of turquoise and gold. “Odd smell.”

Mijnheer Brower rubs his hands. “Silkworms. They have their own odor. It is the mark of quality.”

“Oh, I have smelled silkworms before. This is different. It smells dirty.” Magdalena sniffs. “Like slaves.”

“I can assure you, Magdalena Jansdochter, this cloth was never on a slaver. It was carried on a good clean ship. One of the East India Company boats.”

“That’s what it is!” Magdalena exclaims. “Indian curry! The smell of the brown little men you trade with. It will not wash out, you know.”

I cringe at her cruel words, expecting Mijnheer Brower to protest, but he only sighs. “What price, mevrouw?”

She twirls her feather between her fingers. “One guilder a yard.”

“But it is worth nine!”

“And garlic.” She sniffs. “Is that garlic I detect?”

“Mevrouw, even six guilders a yard would be a loss for me. This is the most precious silk.”

“Very well, mijnheer. I understand.”

"I knew you would, mevrouw. A man must cover his expenses."

"Yes, of course." She rubs her pearl earring. "Well, Cornelia and I must be off now. We hear Mijnheer Hogestyn has a new shipment of silks and we're in a bit of a hurry. But perhaps I should take a quick look at your remnants. Poor Cornelia's gown was caught out in the rain. We slipped in here incognito, but we must have something made up quickly. Show me what you have in reasonably priced remnants."

I glance at her, taken in surprise by her story about my tatters. Are all of her words more subject to her fancy than the truth?

Another turn of the clock, and we are leaving with an agreement that Magdalena's servant will be picking up two lengths of material in the morrow, one of serviceable dark blue bought at one guilder for the lot, the other turquoise and gold, bought at the price of three guilders a yard. Though I slink out of the shop in shame for her meanness, she trips down the porch step, waving her feather in victory.

Dutifully, I say, "Thank you, Magdalena—"

"Sister."

"—*sister,* for the cloth. It has been a lovely day." I sigh, dreaming of the moment I can release my feet from the torture of my shoes and my head from the agony of listening to her manipulations. Not long now, I tell myself, not long.

"Do you think we are going home?"

"I—I thought you might be tired."

"Tired? Me?" She flicks her feather in protest. "Not at all! Such a day invigorates me. Oh, no, no, no, we must go to the dressmaker and get you fitted first."

"But I cannot afford—"

"Hush. Like the cloth, this is my treat." She wrinkles her little nose in a conspiratory smile. "You must look pretty should Mijnheer Bruyningh come through on his offer for dinner." She sees me bite my lip in fear. "But do not worry. Frankly, it was probably just talk. Most of what people say is just talk. Have you not found that to be true, sister?"

She does not wait for my answer.

"You cannot imagine the bargains I make with the dressmaker." Magdalena's laugh is as sweet as the scent coming from the flowerseller's stall. "She knows she must deal or she will not get paid, and something is better than nothing, is it not?"

Chapter 20

Hendrickje at an Open Door.

Ca. 1656. Canvas.

The bells of the Westerkerk have long since rung nine o'clock and crickets chirp into the warm May dark as I trot home from Jannetje Zilver's house. Moeder is in the kitchen when I arrive, peeling away mushy brown layers of rot from an onion by the smoky light of an oil lamp. "I was beginning to worry about you!" she says. "You really should not be out. You avoided any of the streets with P*'s on their houses, didn't you? Mevrouw Bicker says she's heard of two new cases on the Bloemgracht today. That is so close."*

"Jannetje Zilver's street is nice," I say with a sniff as if it were mine. "Jannetje Zilver's moeder says people don't get the plague around there."

Moeder stops peeling for a moment, then with a sigh, continues again. "Are you hungry? I am just getting dinner—I have been waiting for your vader."

"I ate at Jannetje's," I say, watching her pare the remains of the onion into see-through slices. "We had expensive white bread, mince

tart, and asparagus." I look down my nose at the loaf of coarse rye on the table. "Have you ever had asparagus?"

"No. Will you get me the crock of butter, pretty puss?"

"Do not call me pretty puss."

She looks up, surprised, then gets the crock herself. "Will you fetch your vader at the tavern in the park? He must be hungry. Anyhow, curfew is coming, and they are more strict now with the contagion afoot. He should not be out after ten. We don't want any more trouble with the warden."

I skip out into the dark, gladly exchanging the stink of rotting onions, smoke, and paint for the comforting smell of fishy water and wet stone. As I trot over the bridge, a peacock screams from inside the park; something drops into the canal with a hollow plop. Inside the hedges, a fountain sings its watery tune. If only I could find three stuivers, I could go with Jannetje into the maze and finally see that fountain. Moeder is not going.

At the tavern, the screech of a fiddle and rough laughter blasts from the open window as I brace myself for what I know will come next when I enter. Old men smoking pipes will stare; women who don't wear enough over their bosoms will chuck me under my chin; and Vader, in his corner, will drain his tall glass, then rise unsteadily to his feet.

The women will lean against the wall as we pass, giving Vader a look like the one on Moeder's face in a painting he has done of her where she leans against the wall with her bosom uncovered, a key tucked into her bodice. Jannetje Zilver's moeder plays the spinet, takes Jannetje's old clothes to the orphanage, writes letters, tastes the cook's food, scolds the serving girl for leaving a wrinkle in a collar, but Jannetje Zilver's moeder does not have time to slouch against the wall.

A wail, terrible in its length and pitch, pierces the night. I whirl around to scan the row of houses behind me.

The tavern door flies open. I shrink against the painted brick wall as men and women spill outside. A man staggers from a doorway in the row of houses and drops to his knees on the street.

"Our daughter," he groans.

A man steps from the neighboring house. As a crowd gathers, he swings out his lantern, spilling pale light over the man on the ground.

The man with the lantern shrinks back. "Mijnheer Visscher! Get back in your house. Your neck, man!"

The man clamps his hand above his open collar, but not before I have seen the plum-sized swelling in the dim light.

Someone grabs my arm. I look up.

Vader sways in the lamplight. "Don't tell your moeder you saw this. She worries too damn much."

Chapter 21

Tijger sleeps in a patch of sunlight as birds sing outside the open window of Vader's studio. Strains of organ music from the New Maze Park float in on a soft breeze; a woman laughs in the distance. It is a blue-sky day in May, a day for lovers—even the doves are waddling in pairs on the rooftops—and I am stuck inside this musty house, sucking in greasy paint fumes. For twenty-nine days in a row I have been without Carel, a punishment that would be excruciating even without the added misery of having to wear a scratchy old gown the color and weight of a side of fresh-killed beef while Neel Suythof clings to my hand so that Vader can carefully place a tiny dab of paint just right *there*. I can bear no more. I pull my hand away from Neel and rub it.

"Sorry." Neel wipes his own hand on his breeches. "I am holding it too hard."

"It's not you, Neel. It's never you."

Neel casts down his gaze but says nothing. I have hurt him, I am always hurting him, even when I don't mean to.

"It's just that we have been standing here since breakfast," I say, trying to make amends, "and now it's almost time for de noen. Vader, can we please take a rest?"

Vader stands back, regarding his latest dab, then puts down his brush with a frown. I notice with quiet satisfaction that there is but one tiny nick on his chin and that his bristly gray mustache has mostly filled in—my attempts at shaving him have improved over the weeks. "All right, all right," he says, "you may stop."

I stretch my arms as Neel goes to Vader's easel. After twenty-nine days in close quarters with him, I am starting to fear that Magdalena might be right and that Neel cares for me more than he should. Ignore it as I might, the evidence is mounting. To begin, he comes to the workshop earlier than necessary. He sometimes stammers when addressing me. And he looks me in the eye only when forced to, and then on those occasions he turns an alarming shade of red.

Even if he is perhaps a suitable age for a husband—twenty-one to my almost fourteen—his affections are mislaid. I am not serious or sweet tempered enough for him. Kind Neel deserves a porch-scrubbing, sock-knitting, orphan-dressing minister's daughter. I am my rogue vader's coarse spawn—the very reason, evidently, Carel has abandoned me.

"The texture of the skirt is magnificent, mijnheer," Neel says, over at the easel. "I can almost feel it with my eyes."

I wade over in my gown to see for myself, trying not to notice as Neel draws in his breath when I stand next to him. "All this morning we sat for you, Vader, and you only put these three new dabs on it?" I point there, there, and there.

"How did you know that?" Neel says with awe.

Together, Vader and I shrug and say, "Wet paint."

I frown at Vader's grin to keep myself from smiling.

Neel swallows as if recovering himself. "Well, it may be only three strokes, but they have added depth."

Vader nods. "Sometimes a single dab can make all the difference."

"True, mijnheer. A simple reflection of light can bring an eye to life. Light is the key, isn't it?"

I wince, remembering my discussion about light with Carel. How many times in the past twenty-nine days have I recalled that conversation, wondering what I might have said to repel him.

I shake Carel from my head and sigh. "Vader, you haven't even started on the heads and the hands, and my bodice is still just a shadow of underpainting, and yet you have been working on this for over a month!"

"I thank you for your patience," Vader says. "Tintoretto himself could not have asked for a better daughter."

"Who is Tintoretto again, mijnheer?" Neel asks as if I am not in the room.

I cannot help but speak up when I know the answer. "He was a famous Italian artist from the last century. His paintings are quite huge—the size of palace walls—and full of figures and action. His *Paradise* is the largest painting in the world." I tug at the band at the top of my bodice. Hateful thing. My breasts will never blossom forth, smashed like this. I look up and find Vader gazing at me. "What?"

"How did you know about Tintoretto?" Vader says.

I shrug. "I've read your books."

"Which ones?"

"All of them."

Vader beholds me, hands on hips. I look away, suddenly shy.

"Why do you speak of Tintoretto's daughter, mijnheer?" Neel asks.

Vader nods at me. "You tell him."

I smile at the memory of sitting by the front-room window under Vader's book of painters (for it had been nearly my size). How I pored over the stories of the painters' lives, wondering if any of their stories was anything like mine. The closest was that of Tintoretto's daughter—except she was her vader's favorite.

"It is said she was his most faithful assistant," I say, "working with him side by side. They say she had the gift herself—"

Just then, as if struck by an idea, Vader jumps up and hobbles to the canvas on his bandy legs. Carefully, he places a single dab, not listening, it seems, to me.

"I wonder why I have never heard of her," Neel says. "I have been making a study of all the great artists."

"It is because she was a girl," I say bitterly.

Vader leans back to look at his mark. "No, it is because she died young, while her vader was working on the *Paradise*. She became ill as he was finishing his five-hundredth angel, and when she died, he immediately took out his brush and painted her in as the five-hundred-and-first—directly in the center of the piece." He glances at me. "I am surprised you don't remember that part of the story."

I stare at him in astonishment. And he did?

Do not get overexcited about Vader remembering the daughter in the story, I tell myself. He is no Tintoretto. Not only has he not worked with me as Tintoretto worked with his daughter, but he's not painted me, either. When the time comes, he will fill in the face of this painting with Magdalena's fair visage. Far from being the five-hundred-and-first angel, I am but a cut above a straw dummy to him.

I slog over to the window in my gown. No Carel. Of course not. Why do I look, just to wound myself once more? His uncle, seeing me in my shabby clothes, must have advised him against further discourse. Magdalena was right. Nicolaes Bruyningh's invitation was but idle talk, designed to smooth over an awkward situation. Perhaps mere talk is all that Carel's conversation was with me. That is how rich boys must treat inferior girls, speaking to them with honeyed tongues to avoid a confrontation, while the poor girl stupidly mistakes it for love.

When I turn away from the window, Neel snatches up a stone pestle as if he has not been watching me. "Would you like me to grind some pigment, mijnheer?"

"Thank you," Vader says. "I could use some vermilion. Don't thin it too much with the oil. I like a good thick paste, you know."

"Yes, mijnheer."

I could grind and mix pigments just as well as Neel, but would Vader ever let me? "It is a blessing Tintoretto's daughter did not live to maturity," I say. "She would have been disappointed to find that she could not find work on her own."

"Why do you say that?" Neel exclaims, then checks himself. "Perhaps," he says more quietly, "it is harder for them to find the time to pursue it with managing their households and children, but some have done it. In Delft there is a woman artist of the highest caliber, Judith Leyster. She paints, as does her husband. Both are successful in their own right."

Vader puts another painstaking dot of paint on his canvas, then stands back. "I have seen Leyster's work. Family scenes, mostly. Honest work."

I smooth the stiff cloth of my skirt. What if I did try painting but was no good?

"I need to go outside," I say.

Vader waves me off. "Go. I need a break myself. These hands joined together—" He points at the canvas with the padded end of his maulstick. "There's something not true about them."

I shake my head as I pick my way down the steps in my monstrous dress. Could it be because half of the time I am pulling from Neel's grasp? Tenderest love, indeed. Then I smile almost fondly. Poor Neel does put up with much ill use. And I cannot help but ponder his point—does he truly believe a woman might paint?

Engrossed by this thought, I let the organ music, distant shouting, and laughter from the New Maze Park pull me to the front of the house, though I know I should hide my ridiculous costumed self in the courtyard. Across the way, on the ramp into the canal, a crane peers into the water, patient as a preacher, as I settle myself on the stoop. I lift my face to the sun, then close my eyes to watch fireworks of blue against the red of my lids. A peacock sounds its strangled call in the distance. The sun's warmth soothing my cheeks, I listen as water laps against the brick banks of the canal; a moeder duck calls to her young. They answer with endearing peeps as the water laps and laps and laps.

"Remember me?"

I open my eyes. Like a heavenly vision, Carel stands before me in a suit of smooth gray worsted that brings out the shine of his golden hair. He holds out a fragrant bunch of lavender. "Friends?"

The crane flies off with a flap of stately wings as fire leaps into my face. Carel is here! But he calls us "friends."

"What are these for?" I ask, then cringe at my coarseness.

"For you. Hang them in your window, to keep away the contagion."

I mumble something about not worrying about that. How can he appear after twenty-nine days and act as if he has never been gone? I glance down at the lacy layers of my awful vermilion skirt. "This is not my gown!" I exclaim. "I am modeling for Vader." I swallow. "An important work."

He raises golden brows. "Lucky you, watching him paint."

I burst out in a laugh. Across the canal, a grandmother leading her little grandchild turns to look. Carel frowns. I have displeased him.

"Sorry," I say. "It's just that I am . . ." Overjoyed? Furious? Terrified? ". . . weary," I finish.

"I was hoping you could walk."

"I can." I struggle to my feet. "Oh! This terrible gown."

He takes the bunch of lavender, lays it on the porch, then clasps my hands. "*I* think you look like a princess."

"In this?" Oh, *Maidenly Virtures* come to me! I can think of nothing except his hands on mine.

He lets go with a tender squeeze, then walks slowly along the canal, allowing me to breathlessly maneuver next to him in my leaden pool of red. How can he stand me? Why did he return?

"Forgive me," he says.

I cradle hands still throbbing from his touch. "For what?"

"For not coming sooner."

"I understand," I say, though my brain is a tangled ball of yarn.

"It's not like that. I could not come, or I would have been here. I was detained by family business."

"I thought you had . . ." I look away from his iris-blue gaze.

"I did not forget you, Cornelia. How could I forget the girl with the eyes of an artist?"

The death bells of the Westerkerk toll, my heart pounding with them. "There are your bells," I murmur.

"They ring with more frequency. Nine times yesterday. I have heard that three streets over, several families have fallen victim to the contagion. I know all this should trouble me, but instead—each time the bells ring, I find myself thinking of you."

I gaze in the direction of the canal though it is a blur. What is he saying? I swallow, trying to fight my way back down to earth. "So how does your painting come along?"

"I've not had time to paint. I've been put in charge of the family business here while Vader and my older brothers are abroad. You will have to inspire me again."

"You are running the business? What an honor."

He plucks at one of the silky tassels on his collar. "I have no head for it."

"Surely you do."

"No, I don't. Remember those ledgers that I drew upon as a child? I was better off drawing ships in them. The books are a mess. Uncle Nicolaes had been showing me how to enter things, but then he was called abroad, too."

"Oh, he must have gone after we—"

Carel cocks his head. Does he not know his uncle and I have met?

"Excuse me, I am confused," I murmur. How foolish to think Nicolaes Bruyningh would bother to speak of me.

"Uncle Nicolaes and my vader had to track down a man who rented nineteen of our ships and disappeared. Seems his cargo died on all of his ships. He had to throw the entire load overboard."

"Oh, how awful. Cattle or sheep?"

"Slaves. All four thousand sixty-eight of them."

I gasp.

Carel shakes his head. "This man had no insurance to cover his losses and could not pay us, so he skipped off with our ships."

"But—what about all those people?"

"What about them?"

Something inside me snaps to attention.

"Vader and Uncle Nicolaes went to Africa," he says, "thinking their man was hiding there. They were right. Found him roistering on the Gold Coast. They picked him up and a shipload of ivory and tiger skins, too, so they came out for the best. He goes before the magistrate this Friday. I hope he hangs."

I remember the black man Vader painted when I was

little. I can still see his peaceful oyster-pearl eyes, his solid calmness. For just one man like him to go down with a slave ship, let alone thousands of other men, women, and children. I take a breath, then ask, "Does your family often deal in slaves?"

"We don't deal with them at all," he says, pulling back. "That is illegal in Amsterdam. The man who tried to skip from us was English. We just own the ships." He looks at me. "Did you think we would own slaves? That would be so wrong."

"But you own the ships."

"We are not responsible for what our clients put on them. What they carry is on their conscience, not ours."

I shake my head. "I don't understand."

"There is nothing to understand. It's business—just ledgers and abacuses and that sort of boring thing." He smiles. "That is my Cornelia—always thinking of things in an unusual way."

"My Cornelia." He takes my hand, driving all other thoughts from my head, and one by one, laces his fingers between mine. I look up by degrees, past the ebony buttons of his doublet, past his open white collar, past the smooth skin of his neck. His eyes await mine. I swim into their warm blue depths.

Too soon, he says, "I must go."

"But I've hardly seen you."

"Now that Vader is back, there is much to do. I haven't

been to van Uylenburgh's in weeks. Bol has probably gotten another apprentice to replace me."

We start back to the house. The weight of my gown is nothing to me now. "Where do you live?" I ask.

He looks puzzled.

"If I am not to see you for a while, I want to picture where you go."

He laughs. "On the Kloveniersburgwal, then."

"The Kloveniersburgwal?" Moeder's voice drifts into my memory: *It is the name of money.* "I think I was there once with my moeder."

"We are two doors down from the Trip house. Uncle Nicolaes's house is in between. It's not that far from here."

I would not know. The daughter of a bankrupt has no business in that district.

We speak no more. At my stoop, he bends forward to kiss my cheek. My heart roars so loudly in my ears that I cannot hear.

"I will come again," he says into the mad pounding. "Soon. I promise." He picks up the bundle of lavender and places it in my hands. "Hang this in your window. For me."

When he is gone, I wander back to the canal, swishing my bunch of flowers. I spread open my arms. "Hallo, good ducks!"

The moeder steers her ducklings away with a quack. I laugh out loud.

Humming along with the music of the organ, I pluck a

leaf from our tree and throw it onto the brown water, where it is grasped by the current and slowly borne away. With a sigh, I turn to go in. There is movement in the studio window. This time, I see who it is.

Neel.

Chapter 22

Hendrickje.

1660. Canvas.

I am just a little child, but I made her sick. I made her so sad, I made her sick. I wanted to be at Jannetje Zilver's house. Every day that I could, I left Moeder at home so I could see the stained glass windows in Jannetje's front room. I left Moeder at home so I could run my fingers over the twenty-seven sets of collars and caps in Jannetje's linen press. I left Moeder at home so I could play with Jannetje's dolls, her dollhouse, her china tea set. Angry at Moeder for being like Vader, I left her at home, so when the plague came upon her, she was too sad and lonely to chase it away.

"It's pretty puss," I had said when I came home from Jannetje's. Moeder lay on her bed shivering under both my feather bag and hers even though it was July. "Moeder, it's me."

She had opened her eyes, then closed them.

"Moeder, are you ill? Where is Vader? Where is Titus?"

She did not answer. She chattered her teeth and made a noise like a frightening humming.

"Moeder!"

I prayed for her to open her eyes and reach out to me the way Vader had painted her once in a picture, her face so patient and good and forgiving, even after Vader had spent his last guilder on another helmet and I had hounded her without end for a collar like Jannetje's.

But she did not open them.

"Water," she whispered.

A dipper of water was on the floor. I put it to her cracked lips, but the water dribbled down her face. I put my arm around her head and, trembling from the effort, lifted her up. The covers fell from her neck.

Under her ear, straining with all its might to free itself from her skin, was a dark purple goose egg.

A high-pitched scream came from inside me, scalding my throat, deafening my ears. Hands drew me away, and through a red fog of fear, I looked up and saw Vader.

Chapter 23

It is the fifteenth of July, Vader's birthday, but more importantly, two months and ten days after Carel returned to me. Outside the open studio window, the linden tree shimmers in a mild breeze that smells of the sea. The ducklings in the canal have lost their yellow fluff and chase their moeder and each other in their soft new suits of brown as the crane watches them soberly from the bank. Across the way, a plump young moeder holds onto the reins of her toddling baby in his padded hat, while her older son runs along with his pinwheel whirring. All this I can see from where I stand in my colossal gown of vermilion, which now smells distinctly of linseed oil and me. Chiefly me. I can concentrate on none of it. Almost daily Carel has come to see me—Bol has kept him on, thank goodness—though it be for just a few stolen minutes, when he is out purchasing pigments or brushes, delivering pictures to art dealers, or on his way home for the weekend. Even if he could spend hours with me, it would not be enough. I could never get my fill of gazing at him, at the brown-pink swell of his upper lip and the golden hairs on his strong wrists. I am drunk by the sight of him, and now I've been three days without him. I am sick with longing.

"Do I hold your hand too tight?" Neel says.

"What?"

"You looked pained."

I shift under the weight of my skirt, my daydream ended. "It is this gown. I must get my mind off it. Tell me a story, a jest—anything."

"Mijnheer?"

Vader's gaze wanders from his canvas to Neel.

"Does it bother you if we speak?"

Vader slumps back on his stool. "No." He frowns at the ceiling as if directing his complaint to his Friend above. "It seems I have been abandoned, which is rather cruel, it being my birthday." He moves his frown to me. "But keep your pose."

Neel and I glance at each other. Vader has not added a stroke to his painting in two days—he has hardly made progress in weeks—yet day after day we are commanded to remain as statues. How much longer must we wait before he gives up this foolish project? Capturing the essence of tenderest love on a canvas—even as God's own pet, he has asked too much, though his choice of models cannot have helped. If it is burning love he wishes me to demonstrate, he should have Carel holding my hand, not Neel. Now *that* would be a project I could look forward to each morning.

Neel smiles shyly, thinking I am smiling at him. "You really wish to hear a story?"

"Yes. I do."

His face grows serious as he thinks. Tijger strolls in, winds in and out of Neel's legs, then sits at my feet.

"Anything, Neel!" I exclaim. "A tale about wicked stepmothers or talking beasts or the poor growing rich—just tell me something before I go mad!"

"Very well, I have a tale."

"Tell it!"

"It is a true tale."

"Would you tell any other kind, Neel Suythof?"

He grins. "No." In the past few months Neel has lost some of his shyness with me. With Carel visiting so often, I think Neel has given up on whatever interest he had in me, which for some ridiculous reason, makes me sad.

"Well, please get on with it. This dress does not get lighter."

"Very well." The wide golden sleeve of the costume Vader has bid Neel to wear swings as he changes his grasp on my hand. He takes a deep breath. "There once was a blacksmith."

I groan. "A blacksmith?"

"Yes. His name was Quentin Metsys. He was quite skilled at the anvil, skilled enough to leave his home in Louvain for the big city of Antwerp, where he produced intricate works of iron."

Ironworks? He is murdering me. My mind strays to the two wood doves that have landed on the windowsill outside. One plucks at the other's neck. Do birds mate for life? Tijger gets up and stalks toward the window.

"Cornelia?" Neel says. "Are you listening?"

"Yes."

He frowns as if not convinced, but carries on. "Then one day, Quentin delivered one of his finely wrought gates to a stately home on the River Schelde. There, he met a beautiful young maiden. She was the daughter of an artist."

My gaze leaves the doves.

"It was love at first glance. From then on, he could not eat or drink, but would dine on a diet of her smiles."

I look at Neel with interest. A love story?

He stares right back. "He wished her hand in marriage, but her vader would not give his consent. You see, the vader was an artist, a painter of the highest quality, and Quentin was just a lowly blacksmith."

Vader regards his canvas as Tijger sits below the window, his tail swishing. "I believe I have heard this one before."

"What did Quentin do then?" I ask. I think of Carel. "I hope he just carried the girl off."

"No," Neel says pointedly. "He was an honorable man. He would have never gone against the vader's wishes. He decided he would make himself into a man of whom the vader would approve. He would become a painter."

"I thought you said this was a true story," I scoff. Why is Neel telling this?

"It is." Neel looks at Vader, who nods slowly.

"Day and night," Neel continues, "whenever Quentin had a moment's rest from earning his daily bread, he worked with brush and paint, learning from the masters, teaching himself their art. Not a spare moment went by that he did not have his brush in hand, practicing, practicing, practicing.

"Then one day, as he visited the maiden in her vader's studio, he became so intent in their talk that without thinking, he painted a fly on a canvas that the vader had left to dry. Two days later, when the vader returned to his work, he saw the fly, sitting on his canvas.

" 'Shoo!' the Vader cried, whisking at the tiny translucent wings. But it would not move. So he shouted again, 'SHOO!' But the fly would not budge. The vader bent closer to the painting.

" 'Who has done this thing?' he roared."

"Did the maiden tell him?" I cry, then draw back into myself. But who could not help but root for Quentin?

Neel gives my hand an almost imperceptible squeeze. "Her heart breaking with sorrow, for surely the vader would banish Quentin, she answered, ' 'Twas the blacksmith.' "

"Oh, no!" I exclaim.

Neel catches my eye. "Oh, yes. The vader reared back and roared, 'You tell me the blacksmith painted this?'

" 'Yes, Vader,' said the girl."

Just then Tijger jumps, sending the wood doves whirring. Neel does not see him, keen on his telling. " 'Then show me the man,' the vader said. 'I wish to shake his hand. For as surely as I stand here, the man is a painter.'

"And soon after," Neel says quietly, "the two were wed, their hands brought together in marriage by a painted fly." He gazes between Vader and me, then lifts his chin. "That is the end of my tale."

Vader laughs. "Well told!"

Tijger sits in the window and licks his paw as if nothing has happened, but something has, something important and unspoken, for Neel is watching me, waiting for a response.

"You expect me to believe this?" I say. I pull to free my hand.

Neel hangs on. "With my own eyes, Cornelia, I have seen Metsys's face carved in stone, along with an anvil and a palette, on the wall of the cathedral in Antwerp. There is an inscription under it that reads, ''Twas love that taught the smith to paint.'" He lets go of my hand. "Make of it what you will."

I tuck my hands under my arms. "I never knew you were such a storyteller."

Vader puts down his brushes. "'Twas love that taught the painter to tell stories, I would say."

"Vader!" Sweat springs to my brow. "No one is in love here."

Neel's expression loses none of its dignity though his face has turned as red as my dress. "Mijnheer," he says, "I hope you enjoyed my tale."

"Oh, I have, I have, though I am not the one who needs convincing." Vader tosses his palette and brushes on a table. Startled, Tijger stops licking midpaw. "I'm going out," Vader says. "Neel, would you mind cleaning my brushes?"

I follow Vader downstairs, not wanting to be left alone with Neel. "Where are you going?" I demand. Neel has not lost interest in me, why I do not know, and it seems the two have joined against me, in spite of my loyalty to Carel.

"To Titus's. It's my birthday and I wish to see him."

"You cannot go like that."

At the bottom of the steps, he gazes down at his brown painting gown. It is as spotted with dabs of yellow as Tijger's aging belly. Vader shrugs, then takes it off, revealing a green doublet thrice the age of Tijger himself.

"That's no better!"

"I am just going to my son's."

What if he runs into Carel? And I cannot bear for Magdalena to sniff at him in his rags, let alone for me to be left here with Neel.

"Put on your good doublet and breeches and I will shave you."

"I don't want to bother and it's my birthday, so I don't have to."

"Don't you want Titus to be proud of you?"

He clicks his tongue and heaves a sigh. Slowly he shuffles to the back room, where he arranges himself on his bed like a lamb for slaughter. He follows me with pale green eyes red-rimmed with age as I prepare his soap and razor.

"You really should not be so rough on Neel, you know," he says.

"I am not rough on Neel."

"He would treat a woman as she should be treated. That is important, Cornelia."

"I know it is." I come over, then, with an intake of breath, hold down his jaw and pull the razor over his slack cheek. "That is why I am fond of Carel. He treats me like a queen."

He catches some soap sliding down his neck with his shift sleeve as I tap the razor in the bowl of water. "Young Bruyningh," he grumbles. "When are you going to grow tired of him?"

"Never! I would think you'd be encouraging me with him. All those ships."

"I don't give two figs about them."

"I'd think you would. I don't know how else we are going to survive."

"How we survive is my problem. You are much too young to worry about that."

I want to laugh out loud. I have been worrying about surviving my whole life! "Someone has got to worry about how we are to live."

"Pig feathers. When has worry ever changed the course of anything? Anyhow, when you become of marrying age, you should look for a man who will love and esteem you, not who can buy you the most trinkets."

I cannot believe the ridiculousness of this conversation. Vader, the man who would not bother to recognize his love for Moeder under the law, has become an expert on how to treat a woman.

I start to shave him, then stop. Though I would rather swim to New Amsterdam in January, the time has come to face what I do not wish to face. "Vader, why did you not marry Moeder?"

He blinks up at me, a gray, rheumy-eyed lamb, as I stand over him with the razor. "That was between your moeder and me."

I take a deep breath. "Titus told me it was because you would lose all of his moeder's money if you did."

"Is that what he told you?"

I swallow the dry lump in my throat, hoping he will deny it. "Yes."

"Well, it is true that Saskia's last will made it impossible for me to remarry if I wished to keep her money."

"So it was for money!" How can he admit this? Does he not think of how this wounds me? "And it wasn't even enough to keep us afloat."

"You can believe what you need to about your moeder and me. Just remember what I said about Neel."

I take an angry stroke at his cheek. "Neel is an old man."

"He is twenty-one," Vader says calmly for a man with a razor at his throat, "five years younger than Titus, though he is very mature for his age."

I wipe the razor on my rag. "He acts older than you."

"I suppose that is an insult—to whom, I don't know. Both of us, I assume. But I'll disregard it. Let it be on the record that I consider Neel wise for his age."

I rip another path through the soapsuds. "You haven't told me what happened with you and Moeder."

He opens his mouth to reply.

Just then Neel's footsteps ring on the stairs. I feel Vader's eyes upon me as Neel enters, dressed in his street clothes. "Mijnheer, I am off to buy some new pigments." He peers at Vader's face, then smiles at me. "No nicks yet."

"She gets better with age," Vader says. "People do," he says pointedly at me.

"I am not done with you yet," I warn him.

Neel starts to smile, then sees I am not jesting. His face grows sober. "I shall return tomorrow."

Vader waves his hand. "Go. Go. You have my blessing."

I finish Vader in silence, gathering the strength to press him further about Moeder, but before I can get up the courage, I am done and he has put on his best doublet and sleeves and is away.

I wander to the window, where Carel's withered bunch of lavender hangs, and lean on the stone sill. Outside, the youngest van Roop girl runs from our alleyway and into the street, pushing a hoop, as the death bells of the Westerkerk begin to toll, vibrating the stone under my elbows. Over on the Street That Is the Name of Money, does Carel hear them, too? Does he pause at his ledgers and think not of another death, of which there are so many now in the center of town, but of me—of my eyes, of my lips? I push on the lavender, causing it to rain faded blue buds. He cared enough to protect me from the plague—why should I wait for him to come here, when I can do him the favor of going to him? Fie on the silly rules that say the boy must do the courting! I've got legs—I can use them.

"Thank you, Magdalena," I say out loud as I whisk the new dark blue bodice and skirt she has bought me from their pegs on the wall. With speed and care I put them on, dress my hair with the red ribbon I have found in the linen press in the back room, grab my red beads from under my pillow, then take to the street.

The blacksmith's story may not be the only one with a happy ending.

Chapter 24

Hendrickje Bathing.

1655. Panel.

The rain pours down, plastering my hair to my head as I sit on the stoop, my guts pushing and turning, threatening to come up my throat. Behind me, the red-painted P blazes on the door. I can almost feel it burning into my back. On the other side of the door, in the back room, is Vader, shut up with her. He would not bring her out though the man with the cart had come for her. When I had tried to tell Vader the man was waiting, he threw Moeder's red beads at me. At last the man had gone away, the arms and legs of the bodies flopping over the sides of the cart as it bounced over the cobblestones. Now the rain pours down. I stick out my tongue and taste the rain and snot and tears as I push up my sopping sleeve and uncover the red mark on my arm where the beads had hit.

A man comes down the empty street. His hat is pulled down low because of the rain, but there's a bounce to his step and his cape snaps smartly. He carries a pink flower that he shields from the rain with one hand. It's a rose, like the kind in our courtyard. When he tips up his head to look at me, I see his gold mustache.

I stand, the beads clenched in my hand.

Through the curtain of rain, I see him smile as he trots closer. He's grinning as he casually leans to look behind me.

He stops. The rain pours in a curtain between us.

"Who?" he calls, his voice strained.

I open my hand and look at her beads. "Moeder."

I say it, but I do not believe it.

"Hendrickje?"

I glare at him. If he knew her, why didn't he help her? Why didn't anyone help her? Why didn't anyone help me?

Even through the rain I can hear the Gold Mustache Man gurgle like hands are squeezing his throat. He staggers backward, then slipping on the wet bricks, turns and stumbles away.

Slowly, I sit back down. Out in the canal, ducks are floating. They don't care about the rain. In my mind, I see Moeder as Vader once painted her: wading amongst them, wearing only a shift. As in the painting, the white cloth floats around her legs in a filmy cloud. The ducks don't care. They drift past her on the water and sleep.

Chapter 25

Peddlers cry out as I rush past the wooden stalls cluttering the sides of the Westermarkt, on my way to find Carel.

"Hey, aniseed! Aniseed for your stomach pains!"

"Herrings! Sweet as sugar! All fresh! Herrings!"

"Best raisins!"

"See my pears!"

"My carrots!"

"My oranges!"

They would not waste their breath on me if they knew I have not a stuiver.

In the middle of the square, I ask a stringy-haired woman with a tray of wooden toys if she knows where the Trippenhuis might be—surely everyone has heard of the largest house in Amsterdam. Carel lives two houses away.

The woman pulls back with a flap of greasy hair and gives

me a look of disgust. "Do I look like someone who breaks bread with the Trippen?"

I notice her coarse wool sleeves, even more patched at the elbow than my everyday pair, and her dirt-blackened toes peeking from under her dress. "Excuse me, mevrouw."

She waves her hand. "Oh, for heaven's sake, you don't have to look so pitiful. See that street on the other side of the square?" She points toward a group of gentlemen gathered at a street corner, their cassocks folded neatly over their arms. "That'll take you straight to the Dam Square—you can walk it in the time it takes to boil an eel. You will know you're in the Dam when you see the Town Hall. Can't miss it. Biggest building in town, bigger than all the churches—it's got the preachers hopping mad."

I draw in a breath. I was there once, though it has been years. I see my moeder and me, searching through the corridors of the Town Hall, looking for Vader's picture.

"Did you hear me?" the toy lady says.

"Yes, mevrouw. I should go to the Town Hall."

The toy lady frowns like she doesn't believe me. "Good. Then go straight through to the first big street. The Damstraat. Cross two canals, stop at the third. That would be the Kloveniersburgwal." She shifts under the straps of her tray. "You can't miss the Trippenhuis. It's a filthy-big pile. Oh—would you look at that!"

I turn around. The crowd is melting away like sugar in the rain from a woman tapping her way across the square with a large white stick. She holds her son's hand and looks neither left nor right, and no one looks at her.

"I don't care if they give them white sticks or not," the toy lady says. "Family members of plague victims shouldn't be out and about. What, we're supposed to be able to run fast enough when we see the stick? I say keep 'em at home 'til everyone who's dying is dead. We can't afford another big contagion. I lost my moeder, vader, four sisters, and two brothers the last time the plague went through, and I tell you what, I'm not losing no one again. I got my own family now."

I bob my thanks, then hurry on. I will not worry about a new wave of pestilence. Yes, it is making its rounds—Carel's count of the death bells is proof of that—but over the past few months, its toll has kept steady, unlike the year Moeder was carried off, when it spread until every street, every house was filled with wailing. There have been no outbreaks on our street or on Carel's, by his last report. Maybe this contagion will burn itself out, like this woman says, on the few unfortunate families who have caught it, God rest their souls. Surely there can never be a time of plague like there had been before, not now, when I am happy and have Carel and everything to hope for.

I concentrate on more immediate things, like not sweating, a trick in a wool bodice and skirt in the heat of July, and ignore the curious glances of basket-toting housewives sniffing nosegays to ward off the pestilence, and the wink of a man in a pale green cassock. I think of the look Carel will have on his face when I appear at his door. Just imagining his surprise and delight makes me want to squirm with joy.

When I get to the Dam, it is packed with peddlers and lepers and Chinamen and merchants with pomanders around their necks to prevent catching the contagion. Sailors stagger by, smiled at by ladies in bright silks. Dogs sniff among the lot of them, shying away from the horses clopping across the square with their loads. Above it all, looking down calmly like a benevolent rich uncle, is the Town Hall.

I step directly into the path of a drayman's horse.

"Out of the way!" The drayman shakes his whip.

I jump aside with a gasp, then bawl out to a maid carrying a jug, "Which way to the Kloveniersburgwal?"

She points to a street. I stumble away.

A group of people are funneling into the street. I step into the crowd as if I belong there, though my heart is pounding in my ears. What if I can't find Carel? Will I be able to find my way back? Thankful that Moeder's shoes have stretched with the wearing of them, I keep going, over one hump-backed bridge, then another, walking at a furious pace until over the shoulders of the crowd, I see a bridge over a third canal. I fight my way out of the stream of people to catch my breath.

Before me a wide expanse of canal churns majestically under a stately brick bridge. Though the water here is as brown and thick as in our sleepy little canal, the large size, bright colors, and variety of boats sailing upon it give the canal an air of great importance. Through the flapping forest of sails, I can see the five-story mansions lining the street on the other side, the well-groomed twin to the street behind me.

A little boy on a hobbyhorse hobbles toward me.

"Is this the Kloveniersburgwal?" I ask.

He wrinkles his nose up at me then gallops away.

Even children know I do not belong on the Street That Is the Name of Money.

I peer down the brick-paved walkway, then through the jumble of sails on the canal. I realize now that the toy lady had not said which side of the canal the Trippenhuis was on or even which way to go.

The largest house in immediate sight is a redbrick mansion to my right. I set my cap for it, willing Carel to pop from a neighboring door. When I get closer, I can read the sign swinging in the wind above its tall stone entranceway.

THE DUTCH EAST INDIA COMPANY

Not the Trippenhuis. I sag against a hitching post. I will never find Carel. I was foolish to even try. I drift on in the same direction, wondering if I will ever be able to find my way home, when I absentmindedly touch my hair.

My red ribbon is gone.

I am looking for it over my shoulder when someone cries, "Griet! You've come for me!"

An old man reaches out to me from where he sits in the shade of a covered passageway, his knees covered with a hairy blanket. There are other old men, too, sitting on benches, staring blankly.

The old man struggles to his feet and toddles forward. "Bless you, Griet, child!" he bleats, then clings to me with the brittle brute strength of an ancient vine.

I am struggling like a snared rabbit when a firm hand takes my shoulder.

"I am sorry, old friend. Griet has to go now."

I turn and find my face inches from a clean-shaven ruddy jaw. I gasp. Nicolaes Bruyningh?

"Griet!" the old man yelps as Mijnheer Bruyningh untangles me.

"Do not worry, good fellow," Bruyningh says with a tip of his hat, "I shall take good care of her."

The old man nods doubtfully. Mijnheer Bruyningh guides me toward the corner from which I came, his hand like a rock at the small of my back.

"Thank you, mijnheer." I find myself embarrassingly near tears, whether they be from terror or relief or both.

"Poor fellow, I believe he thought you were his daughter." Gently, he asks, "What are you doing here, my dear?"

I swipe at my eye with my knuckle. There is no use in pretending. "I was looking for Carel."

He pushes his hat far back on his head, a gesture that is somehow familiar and comforting. "I see," he says. When he connects with my gaze, I gasp in sudden recognition. Nicolaes Bruyningh is the Gold Mustache Man.

He smiles mildly, not acknowledging my shock. "Unfortunately, it seems our poor Carel has been chained to the desk by his vader. My dear brother has decided Carel must give up his dreams of painting to take up the family business."

"B-but—" I stammer, "Carel is good at painting." Mijnheer Bruyningh acts like I have not recognized him from the past. *Is* he the Gold Mustache Man? Besides no longer having his mustache, he is heavier and much more weathered looking.

Mijnheer Bruyningh gives me an easy grin. "Carel does like to paint. Have you seen his work?"

"No. But I am sure—"

"He was learning, I suppose. One does not master these skills overnight, does one? Though your vader showed his promise early enough."

"Did you know my vader in those days?

He raises eyebrows that glint like golden wires against his reddish skin. "In your vader's youth? Heavens, no." He taps his hat back over his brow. "Do not age me, child—I am your vader's junior by twenty years."

"I am sorry—"

"I met your vader later on."

"Vader did your portrait."

"Yes, he did." I am close enough to see his glance at my beads. "I knew your moeder, too."

I don't know what he wants. Helplessly, I say, "She died

six years ago." If Bruyningh is the Gold Mustache Man, why did he never stop at our house if he knew Moeder and Vader? Why did he just pass by with only a tap to the lips?

Mijnheer Bruyningh gazes at something behind me. I cannot help noticing how much he looks like Carel now that I know them to be related—the iris-blue eyes, the golden hair, the handsome lips. How did I never recognize this before? When he returns his gaze to me, he is smiling. "Well, would you like to see if we can shake our Carel free?"

"Yes, please, mijnheer," I say, though I am so bewildered by Mijnheer Bruyningh's behavior, my only desire is to go home.

"Perhaps it would be best if we went to my house and awaited him. I can send a servant to fetch him."

I slow my pace. Do I know Nicholaes Bruyningh well enough to go to his house without a chaperone? He knows my vader, my moeder, and Titus and Magdalena, and though odd, he seems kind enough. And . . . he is rich.

He turns to me with a schoolboy's grin on his weathered red face. "What would you do if I told you I was the one who ordered your vader's picture recently?"

"You?" I stop. "You ordered the family portrait of the van Roops?"

"Surprised?" He laughs. "Forgive me, but I had to see what your vader was selling these days." He sighs. "I wish it were something closer to what I am collecting."

"I feared it would be too rough," I murmur.

"Truly, he has gotten a bit carried away with his paint."

"Too bad, seeing him squander it all away."

I find myself bristling. "His pictures have a depth you cannot find in other artists' work. He uses the paint for texture."

He regards me for a moment. "I'm sorry, that was thoughtless of me. I should not speak to his daughter in such a way."

I wince. I have spoken out to an important man. What is to become of me? God help me, I am truly my vader's child.

"I just happen to prefer his earlier work," Mijnheer Bruyningh says. "I was hoping he was selling something from his older holdings. Does he keep much stock at home?"

I think of the unsold gallery of paintings crowding the walls of our front room. "Some."

"He used to have all manner of art hanging around his house during the months I came to sit for him," he says. "Mostly his own work, though in his cabinet upstairs he kept copies of the great ones."

Titus had told me Vader was forced to sell everything he owned when he went bankrupt—everything, that is, except for a few precious paintings that he hid from the creditors. It was the collecting of great paintings, rich materials, and natural rarities that drove Vader to bankruptcy, Titus said.

"He's got some pictures," I say.

"Well, if he should ever wish to unload one of his own

older biblical scenes, I would be willing to pay a great deal—if it is the right one for me. I understand that you deal for him now."

I draw back. Because I am a girl and young, I had not thought of myself as Vader's dealer. Perhaps taking the van Roop family portrait to van Uylenburgh qualified me as such. If I am never to paint, maybe I should look into being Vader's dealer. Someone has to take care of our family.

Just then I hear my name being called. I look up.

Carel pushes aside a bunch of herbs and waves from an open window. "Cornelia—is it really you? Hallo!"

My insides leap. The joy and shock and sheer delight on his face is everything I hoped it would be. "Carel!" I wave madly.

"Wait! I shall be right down."

He pops back through the window. Grinning, I remain gazing up at the fine tall house with its rows and rows of freshly painted green shutters. There is a bunch of lavender hanging in every window. So this is where Carel lives. I shrink back in embarrassment when I find Nicolaes Bruyningh watching me.

"Well, now we won't have to fetch the lad, will we?" he says, ignoring my peasant behavior. He bows gallantly. "It was a pleasure speaking with you, my dear."

Suddenly, it comes to me. Before I give it another thought, I put my finger to my mouth and, eagerly watching Nicolaes Bruyningh's hard face, tap my lips three times.

Other than a blink of golden lashes, his face is coolly blank.

Heat leaps to my cheeks. He must think me mad, tapping away at myself like a monkey with an itch. "Excuse me, mijnheer. I thought—It's just that . . ."

He smiles, but there is a chill in it that warns me to continue at my own risk.

I want to slump to the bricks. How had I ever thought Mijnheer Bruyningh could be the Gold Mustache Man? The Gold Mustache Man disappeared with the plague—probably one of its victims, like so many others. And now here I am, ruining any chance of the good opinion of Carel's esteemed uncle. I sink into miserable silence until Carel comes bounding out the door and breaks our awkward quiet. Still, as Carel leads me away, chatting about events in his day, I cannot but wonder how much damage I have done.

Chapter 26

The July sun beats down upon us as we walk along the Street That Is the Name of Money. Though people crowd the spotless brick walkways, it is strangely quiet. Ladies, sniffing silver pomander balls filled with rose petals and herbs, stroll by with a faint swish of silks, their barefoot African servant boys waving ostrich-feather fans behind them. Into their rose-scented wakes stride men in groups of two and three, speaking in hushed tones. Meanwhile the water in the canal discreetly laps the stone banks as boats, filled with money-making cargoes, sail solemnly by. Only a man in daffodil satin breaks the hush, with the spritely clopping of his dapple gray mount. My street on the Rozengracht, with its oily smell of pancakes and its din of jolly organ music and shouting people, though less than a mile off as the rook flies, is a world away.

Carel is spreading his hands in disbelief. "Vader lost the whole stake he put into my apprenticeship. Two hundred fifty guilders—and he did not bat an eye! He told Bol I was joining the family business and that was that, no matter what I said. I told him, 'Very well, Vader, but why did you not say this before I'd spent three years learning the craft?' "

I pull my gaze away from a small African boy struggling to keep a fan nearly as large as he is aloft over a pinch-faced old woman in a wagon-wheel ruff. Though slaves are not allowed in Amsterdam, Africans still find their way into households as servants. I think of the several thousand African slaves Carel said were lost at sea on his family's ships. With a sigh, I force the terrible image away. Carel no more represents his vader than I do mine.

Carel looks at me expectantly. It is my turn to add to his conversation. "Why did your vader change his mind about your painting all of a sudden?" I ask.

"He said he thought I'd grow out of my whim to be a painter, and now that they need another hand in the business, he wasn't waiting any longer. It was time I did something practical."

I could not argue with that. How many times did I feel the pinch of Vader following his art? But if Carel gave up painting, would he also give up me?

"What if you practiced painting in your spare time?" I ask.

"What spare time? Vader's worse than Bol. He works me to a nub—without pay." He looks over his shoulder. "Just you wait—he'll send his man out after me in a moment. I'm sorry, but I won't be able to walk you home."

"No matter, I can find the way."

He sees my face and laughs. "Don't look like that—I want to walk you! I just can't."

"I know," I murmur, though I cannot help but doubt him. I look back over my shoulder at the banks of green shutters on his princely house. Why has he never taken me there? Even now, he leads me away from it. I pull him away from my house because I am ashamed of Vader, but does Carel pull me away from his because he is ashamed of me?

"There must be some way you can keep painting," I say, ignoring the hollowness in my gut. "It is your dream." And his only tie to me.

He touches my hand. "Only you acknowledge that. What would I do without you?"

When I search his eyes, he will not look away.

"Don't worry," he says, "I'm still coming to see you, no matter what they say. Vader sends me on errands—I'll sneak out then."

"If you do come—"

"Not if. When."

"When you do come, you can paint at my house. We have everything you need. You don't have to give it up, Carel." Nor me.

He kisses my hand. "This is why you are so special to me."

My head seems to be floating as I gaze at the golden down above his upper lip, then up into his laughing blue eyes. I will do anything to keep you, Carel Bruyningh. Anything.

Though almost suppertime when I return home, everything is as it was when I left, except that Vader's cheeks are already peppered with white. He is in his studio, standing before his would-be portrayal of Tenderest Love.

"Hallo, Vader." I try to hide the smile that has been on my face since I left Carel.

He glances over his shoulder, then back at the painting. He doesn't ask where I've been.

"I've been out getting some cheese for supper." I put the tray I had quickly made up for him on his worktable then retreat toward the window. "Eat."

He lifts his hands. "Why do you abandon me, God? I studied Titus and Magdalena all afternoon and still you gave me no sign. Where were you leading me when you gave me this idea? I am lost now." He goes to the table, tears off a chunk of bread, and chews absently.

I scan his table with its clutter of pig bladders filled with paint, hog-bristle brushes standing in jars, and dirty paint-knives. It would be easy for me to tuck a few things in my apron for Carel to paint with when he next comes. Maybe I should start collecting things gradually—a bladder of bone-black paint here, a paintbrush there. Then I would be ready when Carel comes, giving him a reason to return, for surely his family will not make it easy for him to visit. Just the thought of Nicolaes Bruyningh's cool face when I tapped my lips makes me cringe. *He* will not encourage his nephew to mix with me. Whatever made me make that silly sign? Now I will never be able to prove to him that I am good enough for Carel.

I draw in a breath. "Vader, you knew Nicolaes Bruyningh. What was he like?"

Vader swims out of his fog. "Bruyningh?" His pale green eyes bore into mine. "Why do you want to know?" he says sharply.

Blood rushes painfully to my cheeks. "He's Carel's uncle."

Vader crosses his arms. "Oh, this is about the nephew, is it?"

I dust off the windowsill with a corner of my apron.

"I had hoped this would resolve itself on its own, but evidently it has not. I am going to have to ask you to stay away from the nephew, Cornelia. I know he's been lurking around here off and on for the past few months, but I can no longer cast a blind eye to it. If he comes, you aren't to see him, do you understand?"

I gape at him in disbelief. After years of neglect, he advises me now? "You cannot tell me this!"

"Oh, yes, I can. You are to have nothing more to do with that clan."

"Why?" I demand. "Because they're rich?"

He scowls.

My voice drips with disdain. "I happen to know that they are very nice. Even Nicolaes."

" 'Nicolaes?' " The alarm in Vader's voice startles me. "Have you spoken with him?"

I am glad I have changed back into my everyday clothes. If I'd been in my good dress and with my guilty, furious face, he would be sure to know the truth, that I am fresh from the Street That Is the Name of Money.

"Tell me, Cornelia, how do you know him?"

"I must go wash the linen now." I start away from him, rattled by his rapid change in moods and my own anger.

"Cornelia!"

I shrug bitterly. "He is just Carel's uncle."

"I'm telling you!" he calls after me. "Stay away from those Bruyninghs."

Something in Vader's voice makes me turn around. Even in my anger, his anxious face frightens me, and then I am all the more angry for having been frightened. "Why?" I exclaim. "Moeder would want me to be part of such a rich family. She hated being poor."

He blinks as if slapped. Slowly, he lowers himself onto his cross-legged chair. "She did, didn't she?"

"Yes."

His shoulders sag. "I would like to think that is not the same as hating me."

"I'll come back for your tray," I say, then escape to the kitchen, where a pile of soiled linens and dirty pots awaits me. I snatch up a bucket, march out to the courtyard, and throw myself into pumping. Why does Vader wish to keep me from

Carel? Instead of wanting me to be happy, he tries to make me miserable, and he succeeds, oh, he succeeds. It is so very like him to not consider my feelings.

But, as I continue to murder the pump handle, my arms aching and my lungs burning, the image comes to my mind of the nervous, almost-frightened expression on Vader's face when he ordered me away from the Bruyninghs. Something about them upsets him greatly, more than just Carel courting his daughter. Since when does Vader care that much about me? If anything, he should be delighted a rich boy has taken an interest in me. He was certainly proud when Titus wed Magdalena and her money.

I watch the water spouting into the almost full bucket. Whatever it is that troubles Vader about the Bruyninghs, there will be no asking him. Vader is as a closed book to me. He will remain upstairs, abandoned by his God and me, an old man with his paints, and I will stay downstairs with my washing, my books, and my cat. We will exist in the same dwelling but will live alone, though nothing separates us but some damp walls, our pride, and our past.

I wipe my eye on my shoulder, then, with a sigh, haul the splashing bucket into the house.

Chapter 27

More than a month has passed since Vader banished Carel, and it is a warm afternoon in late August. I sit back on my heels at the base of our stoop and wipe the sweat from my forehead as soapsuds drip from my scrub brush and down my arm. How the other housewives on our street can stand scouring their stoops each day just for the purpose of getting them clean is beyond my reckoning—even without the ordinance to keep one's housefront clear of debris to prevent the sickness, it is Dutch custom to do so. However, until five weeks ago, it was not *my* custom. Our stoop could have been three feet deep in duck drek for all I cared; I have taken up scrubbing it only in case Carel has snuck away from the family business.

For sneak here Carel does. He does not know that only a coincidence provided the means to keep us together. He does not know that the day after Vader laid his foot down about my seeing Carel, I was in the front room rereading *Maidenly*

Virtues when I heard a blood-chilling scream just outside our door. When I ran to see who had been stabbed or possibly strangled or succumbed to the plague, I found Titus on the porch step with Magdalena, who was holding up her spaniel's paw and shrieking as if it had been severed.

"Ducks!" she accused at a shout.

Upon quick examination of paw and porch, it became clear that the duck family had paid our stoop a visit and that Precious, the spaniel, had accidentally trod in their leavings. *Sorry,* Titus mouthed, when it also became clear that Magdalena would not be satisfied until I got down on my knees with bucket and suds and scoured the stoop that very instant. It was when Titus and she were inside comfortably visiting with Vader, that I looked up from my angry scrubbing and saw Carel coming down the street.

With a jolt of joy, then guilt, then determination, I flung away my scrub brush, smoothed my hair, and ran to him before he could get within sight of our house. We stole away toward the Westerkerk, holding hands and laughing, he because he felt he was tricking his vader, and I because I felt I was tricking mine.

Since then, learning that two in the afternoon is the hour of his vader's nap and the time Carel is likely to steal off, my scrub brush and I have kept our appointment with the stoop. Carel does not always manage to escape to come to see me, but often enough to keep my dreams full of his luscious lips and dancing eyes. He has not yet asked me why I always run from the house to meet him—indeed, why I've become so enamored of scrubbing of late. Perhaps it has not occurred to him that a failure like Vader would disapprove of a rich man's son like he. Perhaps that is for the better.

Now, I am about to resume my irksome but possibly rewarding scrubbing when I see someone walking along the canal. I sit up, my pulse quickening, to peer closer, then slump back on my heels. It is only Neel, walking along the canal, his head down as if he thinks to solve the problems of the world. Even as he nears, he seems not to see the brilliant blue of the late-August sky this afternoon or the ducklings, now the size of their moeder, squabbling in the canal, or the brown edges that have appeared on the heart-shaped leaves of the linden tree. He walks as a man lost in thought . . . and then he sees me. His somber face brightens in a smile so dear I find that I am moved.

"Hallo," he calls.

I am not being loyal to Carel, smiling like this. "Hallo." I make myself frown.

Neel's smile falls, too.

He stops at the bottom step, then clears his throat. "I had hoped you might have some time to model for my picture today."

I look down the street. "I had better finish these steps." I dip my brush into my bucket. I am so used to talking to Carel about his painting, which he carries on in secret in his uncle Nicolaes's attic, that I ask, "Which picture?"

"The Prodigal Son."

"Oh." I think of the cast in the story—the vader, the young returning wayward son, the good older son who stayed at home. I cannot think of any girls in the story. "Who am I to be?"

"The elder brother," he says.

"Flattering."

"I did not mean to imply you look like the elder brother, I only need you to hold his position."

"I know." You cannot jest with the boy. "So it sounds like you have figured out where you want to place him in the picture now."

Neel looks pleased that I have remembered the point that has been troubling him in his picture. Truly, it is just that I am used to discussing work in progress with Carel. It is what Carel and I enjoy talking about. I know Carel's favorite color: lapis lazuli (because it matches his eyes). I know his favorite painter: Ferdinand Bol (because so many of Bol's paintings hang in the Bruyningh house and Bol was his teacher). I even know which dealer supplies the brushes he favors: Jan van Pelt, on the Spui. Carel had given me money to buy him three hog-bristle brushes there, which I did when he was setting up the studio his uncle so kindly provided for him.

"When you get a chance," Neel says, "I would welcome your opinion on where I am putting the brother in the composition."

I glance down the street. "Very well. When I come in."

"Of course."

I look up at him when he does not go away.

"Cornelia, why is it that you never paint?"

My mouth slides open. I wobble on my heels.

"It just does not make sense to me," he says, his forehead puckered in earnestness. "You have a wonderful eye, you know all there is to know about technique from watching your vader, and you obviously have a great passion for it. Why don't you do it yourself?"

I feel my face burn with embarrassment. "I don't know," I mumble.

"Forgive me for speaking out," he says. "I did not mean to trouble you." He turns to go.

"No, not at all." I rise to my feet. I am so used to talking about other people's painting, it is a new sensation to be in the spotlight, an agreeable one.

He starts to walk away.

"Where are you going?" I ask.

"To the courtyard door," he says over his shoulder.

"Why?" Oh, why doesn't he stop?

He turns and smiles at me gently. "So as to not soil your clean steps."

After he is gone, I slowly return to my scrubbing. Neel is right—why do I not paint? As he says, I have been brought up in the studio—whether Vader liked it or not—and know enough to try my craft. And if Neel is right about the successful woman painter Judith Leyster, my sex shouldn't hold me back. If she can sell her work, so could I. But what if I try and am awful? What if people laugh at the poor doodlings of foolish Rembrandt's foolish daughter?

"Hallo, my little housemaid."

When I look up, Carel is beaming down upon me. "Drop your brush. Let's go for a walk."

Chapter 28

I secretly smooth my hair and skirt as Carel and I stand along the Bloemgracht, the Flower Canal, just to the north of my canal, waiting for the death bells of the Westerkerk to finish their solemn tolling. We have run there from my house—"to get away from prying eyes," as I told him. Now seagulls wheel over the step-gabled houses. A man rows by in a boat stacked with hides. At a shallow place in the canal made by a ramp into the water, a crane wades, carefully searching for fish.

At last the bells stop. "That is the first the death bells have rung this week," Carel says into their echo. "Over by my house, the funeral bells of the Old Church have sounded just once in the past two days. Do you know, Cornelia, I think the contagion is loosening its grip." He throws a stone at the crane. It lifts elegant wings and flies off, unconcerned.

"Touch wood," I say, then rap on a barrel at the canal's edge for luck.

"You told me not to worry," Carel says. "I should have listened to you."

"What good does worry do? Has it ever changed the course of anything?" I frown at my words. I am beginning to sound like Vader.

"You're right, as usual. How did you ever get such a good head on your shoulders? The girls Vader has introduced me to—" He stops when I make a face. "Don't worry. It is just at church. He is always trying to force some girl upon me. This week it was Hendrik Trip's niece, Amalia. All the silly thing could do was laugh."

"Oh."

"You, you never laugh like a fool. You're serious."

I think of Neel's solemn face. "Hardly attractive."

"I find it so." He kisses my fingertips. I sigh with happiness.

He frowns at something over my shoulder. "Your cat has followed us again."

I turn around. Tijger is rubbing himself against a barrel. I grin, pleased at my dear pet's devotion.

Carel pushes him with his foot. "Shoo."

Tijger leaps out of kicking distance, then sits down. My heart goes out to him.

"Are you sure you should keep that old cat?" Carel says. "Maybe the contagion is lessening, but still, as a precaution . . ."

"None of us have gotten sick yet," I say, hurt, in Tijger's defense. I think, with a twinge, of my moeder. It is true, I did have Tijger when she fell ill. Still, none of the rest of us had caught the contagion, as Titus had pointed out not long ago, and we remain healthy now.

Carel crosses his arms. The tassels of his perfectly white shirt ride on his strong chest as he heaves a sigh. "I am having trouble with my self-portrait."

"What is the matter?" I say, glad that the subject has changed.

"My nose. I cannot get it right. It looks like a wedge of cheese."

"Noses must be hard to do—they are all shadow." I give it a moment's thought. "I would think you need to keep in mind the source of light in your picture at all times."

"Yes, of course. You are absolutely right." He laughs. "Light is always the key, isn't it?"

"That's what they say." I float a tentative look his way. "Maybe I should try painting and see for myself." I pause. "I've never actually tried it, you know."

"Really?"

I shake my head.

"You should try it. You'd be good."

"Do you really think so?"

"Of course. Anyhow, Uncle Nicolaes says my painting goes well. He asks when you are going to come and see it."

"He does?"

"You act surprised."

"I did not think he liked me."

"Of courses he does. Who wouldn't?" He squeezes my hand. "Besides, he is a good man. It is just like him to let me paint in his attic. Sometimes I think he is more of a vader to me than my real vader is."

"You are lucky to have him," I say, then sigh. Perhaps my painting is not such a good idea after all. Perhaps I am lucky he didn't ask any more about it. As *Maidenly Virtues* says, women of breeding do not exert themselves unduly. Still . . .

The carillon bells of the Westerkerk jangle merrily in the distance. "Three o'clock," Carel says as a seagull splashes into the canal. "Vader will be waking. I need to go." He kisses my fingers again, then pulls back to look at them. "Rough. What have you been doing to your hands?"

I am still rubbing my fingers against my lips, wondering what ointment I can make to smooth them now that daily scrubbing has coarsened them, when I trudge up the stairs to the studio. There, Neel mixes pigment into linseed oil while watching over the shoulder of Vader, who is working on his own self-portrait. Vader had started it just days ago, and unlike the Portrait of Tenderest Love, it comes along quickly. Already the face of a stubborn old man stares proudly out of the canvas.

"You capture yourself well," I say, nodding toward the picture.

Vader looks in the mirror, then transfers a dab of paint

from his palette to the canvas. "Every decent painter can portray himself well. In fact, he puts himself in every painting, whether he likes it or not. It is really amusing when he strikes upon the creature that resembles him best. My student Carel Fabritius looked exactly like a finch he painted, and young Bol was the spitting image of the spaniel he'd done."

"I have heard of this sort of thing," says Neel, stirring his mixture. "Some say that Leonardo da Vinci's famous portrait of the mysterious lady is actually a painting of himself. He gave her his features."

"Hmm." Vader places another spot of paint. "Perhaps he thought of himself as a woman."

"So that is why Vader painted that carcass of beef when I was little," I say. "He paints himself."

Vader and Neel turn in unison to look at me. Vader bursts into a laugh.

"Cornelia," Neel says. "Be kind."

"No," Vader says. "She's got a point. At the time I was painting it, I did feel rather like a butchered carcass. It was at the time of my bankruptcy, when my creditors were coming at me from all quarters."

I wince and glance at Neel to gauge his disapproval at Vader's poverty, but he only tips the pot he is stirring toward Vader.

Vader peers inside it. "Put in more thinner."

Neel lifts his chin when he sees me watching. "So, Cornelia, how would you see me? As what creature should I paint myself?"

I look into his solemn face and find myself smiling.

"As a crane."

"Sorry, boy," Vader says with a laugh.

Neel looks away with a small, pained smile.

"It's not an insult," I say in a rush. "Cranes are noble in their movement and they show great patience while hunting fish. They move unmolested by other birds or beasts, and they have beautiful"—I notice them both staring—"wings." I clamp my mouth shut.

Neel lowers his head. But when he looks up, and our eyes connect, it is I who must look down. What has gotten into me?

Vader looks between Neel and I, then presses back a smile. "Well, Neel, how is the work coming along on your Prodigal Son?"

Neel breathes in. "Slowly, mijnheer."

Even though I dare not look at Neel, I can feel something in the air between us. Confused, my gaze seeks something safe—his unfinished painting, propped against its easel. One shadowy figure is kneeling, another standing over it, another looking on.

Vader is studying it, too. "Where is the scene supposed to take place? I have no sense of it."

Neel lets out a breath. "I had thought a rich palace."

"You don't say," Vader says. "I can't see it. Maybe some props would help get you going. Cornelia—go look in the attic. See if there's something in there that will inspire him."

I leave, grateful to get out of the room. What is wrong with me, babbling about Neel and cranes? Neel is boring, dull, and serious. I do not find him attractive. Just because he had suggested that I paint, I make too much of him.

Once inside the attic, the dusty air brings me back down to earth. I scan the shrouded piles before me, my nose adjusting to the smell of tar and mold and my eyes to the quiet gloom.

A loud *bong* vibrates the room. I jump.

I pat my chest, calming myself. It is just the hateful death bells. So they ring again today. Well, that signifies nothing. Carel is right, the contagion is abating, I tell myself, then try to remember where I'd once seen a vermilion and gold carpet among this mess. Perhaps the kneeling figure in Neel's *Prodigal Son* can rest upon the rug, suggesting the rich palace Neel mentioned.

I inch past a pile of rotting trunks to prod a rolled-up length of material with my toe. When it does not open, I bend down and lift an edge. It is not the carpet, but a canvas. I unroll it until I am greeted by the one-eyed stare of Mijnheer Gootman.

I smile to myself.

Gently, I roll the canvas back up, then stand, bumping my head. I whirl around and see an empty birdcage swinging from the rafters like a tolling death bell. In its arc I see a painting from which a drape has fallen.

I squeeze my eyes shut but it is too late. I can see the painting as clearly as if my eyes were open. I can see the dark shadow between her legs. Her uncovered breasts. The red ribbon winding down her neck like a snake. The string of red beads in her hair. Moeder's face is turned to the side.

Why did you let Vader paint you like this? He spared you nothing, not a ripple or blemish, not your belly, not the sorrow on your face. He left you exposed for anyone to see, and you let him. You let him.

"Bird?"

Titus is in the doorway.

"What are you doing here?" I bolt to him before he can see the painting. She is not his moeder. He has no right.

"Well, I can always count on a warm welcome from my little sister."

I herd him out the doorway and shut the door. "What *are* you doing here?"

"That's not much more hospitable, Bird. But never mind. Magdalena waits downstairs. We have some news to share."

He steps down onto the landing and opens the studio door. "Vader? Oh, hallo, Neel."

Soon all but Neel have gathered in the front room, where Magdalena sits on the chair with the lion's-head arms, her silvery hair looped high on her head like a crown, the peach silk of her dress pouring down her lap in shimmering folds. With pale almond eyes she looks down upon us crowded before the printing press and worktable, smiling as at small children.

Titus says, "We wanted you to be the first to know—"

"After my mother," Magdalena says.

"—that Magdalena is with child."

Vader springs forward and hugs Titus, then Magdalena, then Titus again. "Oh, this is excellent news!"

Magdalena receives my embrace with a patient smile.

"According to the physician," Titus says, wheezing in Vader's renewed hug, "the baby is due in March. It will be a boy."

"You know all this?" Vader says.

"We have the very best physician in Amsterdam," Magdalena says. "Hendrik van Roonhuysen. Johanna de Geer recommended him. He has delivered her of all her children."

"But how do you know it's a boy?" I ask.

"Because," Titus says with a grin, "in my bones I feel lucky."

Vader shakes Titus's hand. "May your child bring you the happiness you've brought me."

I frown at Titus. Sweat clings to his brow and upper lip. "You look hot. Are you well?"

"It is the end of August," Magdalena says. "Everyone is hot. He is not the one carrying a child."

Titus reaches over and pats her hand. "That is right. I will not complain."

We chat for a few minutes, discussing names for the baby until Magdalena states it will be named Jan after her vader, period; then we listen in detail to how Magdalena is feeling. At last she rubs her belly, which has not begun to round, and says, "We must be off, Titus sweet. I shall need a nap soon. We were on our way to the lacemaker's shop," she explains. "I am working on our son's christening gown."

I cast a look of sympathy to Titus but he does not catch it. He wipes his forehead with the back of his arm. "I am sorry, Magdalena, but I don't know what's wrong with me. I am so very hot."

"Sympathy pains," Magdalena says lightly. She kisses his hand, then draws back with a not entirely playful smile. "You are a sweaty beast!"

"I think I need to go home and lie down."

"But we have come all this way," Magdalena says plaintively. "I had my heart set on finding the perfect Flemish lace for Little Jan's gown."

"Neeltje," Titus says, "could you go with her? Magdalena, would you mind?"

Magdalena scowls, then spreads her hands with generosity. "Of course not. Change quickly, Cornelia," she says, eyeing my clothes. "I shall wait."

Chapter 29

"Dear Titus!" Magdalena says as we stroll down the street on the far side of the Westermarkt, the peach silk of her skirt swishing. "He is such a child. I am supposed to be the queasy one." She raises her sweet voice to a shout above the din of the peddlers and their haggling customers. "For several weeks I was so tired I thought I was sure to die—I had Titus fetch the minister, and Moeder was up nights brewing me potions—but I have since shaken that malaise and feel quite marvelous." Her pale eyes flash at a carter who has gotten too close with his wagon heaped with hay. "Are you blind?" she shouts. "You almost killed us!"

The carter yanks on his reins, jerking back his horse's head. Hay slides off the top and onto the street. I stop to pick it up.

Magdalena pulls me away by the arm. "I am the stronger one of Titus and I," she says over the marketplace din. "Women are always the stronger sex." She smiles to herself. "The trick is not appearing to be so."

I falter as we walk. Have I been appearing to be too strong to Carel? I should have never, ever mentioned I wanted to paint to him. He will think me in competition with him. And I am always spouting off my opinions. Does he think me bossy?

The noise lessens as we leave the Westermarkt. As I worry about chasing Carel away with my pushiness, Magdalena continues to list Titus's many faults as we journey down narrow streets and across humpbacked bridges. Soon we enter Dam Square, where the sounds of laughter and clopping hooves and the creaking of carts mercifully drown out Magdalena's complaints. I gaze at the Town Hall, remembering, all of the sudden, going there with Moeder to look for Vader's picture. I remember seeing the men come with the cart when we returned home, and Vader raising his knife—

"Cornelia?" Magdalena peers into my face. "Cornelia, are you listening?" She pulls back with a swish of silk when satisfied she has my attention. "Do you see that third building to the left of the Town Hall? The pretty one, with the silver sign?"

"Yes."

"That's the Silversmith's Guildhouse. When I was a child, my vader was the head of the guild. I imagine Little Jan shall be someday, too."

"You don't think Titus will want his son to deal in art with him—when he gets that business going better?"

"Oh, dear, no. It does not pay, does it? In fact—you

mustn't tell your vader, this is still a secret—Titus is taking silversmithing lessons from my uncle."

"He is?"

"He seems to have quite a knack for it. He made me the sweetest candlesticks. He had engraved flowers on them. I keep them at our bedside."

The candlesticks he had offered to me—dear Titus, had he tried to give them to me first?

She shades her eyes to look across the crowded square. "You will have to keep in mind this lacemaker when you next need lace. I know, I know, it is ladylike to make one's own lace, but Johanna de Geer does not make hers. It is a waste of her good time, she says. A waste of mine, too. Goodness knows I have plenty of other things to do."

Magdalena has a cook, a maid, and a moeder to jump to her every command. I wonder what those other things to do might be, besides to harry my brother.

"This woman makes lace far better than I can," Magdalena says. "Of course she does. She is only a thousand years old. She has been at it so long she probably weaves all those threads as easily as breathing. Besides, Johanna has told me how to get a bargain from her."

Magdalena trods near a legless beggar, who, quick on his hands, skitters crablike out of her way. "The secret, Johanna says, is to buy more than you need at a cut-rate price."

I pull my apologetic gaze from the angry beggar.

"Later," Magdalena says, "you bring back what you don't

need for a refund at the regular price. You come out ahead that way, you see."

"But—isn't that wrong?"

"No. The old woman builds a high profit into her price. I am just bringing it down to a reasonable rate. She should not charge so much in the first place."

We leave Dam Square by way of the Damstraat. I recognize where we are—headed toward the Kloveniersburgwal.

Magdalena nods at a young woman dressed in pink silk with bows all over the skirt and trailed by a small brown-skinned boy in a matching livery. He struggles along on his tiptoes, balancing the long handle of a pink umbrella in an effort to keep her shaded.

"I asked Titus to get me one of those," Magdalena says after they have passed. "But he is being rather stingy and refuses to. Johanna de Geer has one. Named Coco. A darling little thing from the New World. Quite rare, you know. He had an unfortunate habit of sucking his thumb—not really nice for serving at table—but she cured him by putting red East Indies pepper on his nail."

My heart sinks for the little boy, so far from home without a moeder. What is wrong with Magdalena, not realizing he is not a toy or a pet but a feeling, frightened child? "What happens to the little boys when they grow up?"

Magdalena blinks her almond-shaped eyes. "I do not know. I had not thought of that." She laughs. "Now I know why Titus calls you Worry Bird. I shall call you the same."

She pauses a moment at a street corner and presses a slender finger to her lips. "Now, where are we?"

My heart beats harder. What if we see Carel? What foolish blunders will I make around him with her judging my every move? Has Vader told her and Titus that I'm not to see him?

"Are we going to Kloveniersburgwal?"

"No," she says, "the street before it. The shop is quite convenient to Johanna's house. Why do you ask?"

I shake my head.

"Oh, I know." She gives me a sly smile. "It is the Bruyningh boy, isn't it?"

I look down.

"Wor-ry Bird!" she sings.

I bite my lip.

"There's no use in denying it. People talk, you know. A person cannot sneeze in this town without everyone knowing it."

I gasp. "What did Vader say?"

"Your vader? Nothing that I know of."

"Someone else is talking? What could they possibly say?"

"Oh, just that you two young people are keeping company. Nothing much. Johanna mentioned it to me—Carel's vader has been grumbling."

"Carel's vader is grumbling!"

Her pretty face clouds. "Maybe I ought not to tell you."

"Please do. You must!"

"It's just that, well, Carel's vader does not approve."

My gut turns to stone. "He does not approve of my vader."

"No, actually he respects your vader. Your vader is actually quite famous, you know. Everyone still speaks with wonder of *The Company of Banning Cocq*, odd as that painting was with all the commotion in it. What in the world was a girl with a *chicken* doing in the middle of a company of shooters?" She shakes her silvered ringlets in amusement. "Regardless, it is common knowledge your vader has been sought out by princes from both here and abroad."

I find I am starved for her words of praise about Vader. "Princes?"

"The Stadholder himself, for one, and just last year, the Florentine prince, Cosimo de Medici."

I remember a group of men in slashed sleeves and feathered hats appearing at our door last December, but as they had left without purchasing one of Vader's pictures, I had put them out of my mind. Could it truly have been a prince and his men? If only it were true that Vader was not a laughingstock! I could hold my head high and claim my place with Carel.

"Now, to be sure, everyone thinks your vader is the tiniest bit odd, but that is the artist's lot, is it not? Part and parcel with the lifestyle. There's a new young artist in Delft, Jan Vermeer, who paints his wife, daughters, and maid, all doing absolutely nothing. It is like painting dust gathering! Titus thinks his work great, but I find him quite mad. This is why I won't have my little Jan take up the brush—too many oddbodies in the trade. But the problem with Mijnheer Bruyningh does not lie with your vader."

I look at her.

She smiles sadly, as if she is most sorry for me. "You should never listen to what people say. I understand your moeder was very sweet."

The meaning slowly sinks in. "You mean, Carel's vader does not approve of my moeder?"

She waves her hand. "Put it out of your mind."

But I cannot. I feel the sting of it during our visit to the lacemaker, a grandmotherly woman from Bruges whose kind attempt to show me different lace patterns does nothing to shake the sick feeling in my gut. Soon we are off with a large bundle of lace—much too much for a baby's gown—and though I feel badly for the lacemaker, at least we are going home, where I can hide and lick my wounds. But instead of turning for home, Magdalena leads us toward the Kloveniersburgwal.

"Where are we going?" I ask in a panic.

"I would like to drop in on Johanna," she says.

"Johanna de Geer?" Just down the street from Carel's house? "But—I am not dressed properly!"

"Is that dress I had made for you not to your liking?"

I look down on my plain dark garb. "I love it, but—"

"Wor-ry Bird!" Magdalena says. "Do not fear seeing Carel or his vader. We shall duck into Johanna's without anyone being the wiser. Who are those Bruyninghs to us, anyway?"

We continue toward the Trippenhuis. I try to slow my step

but Magdalena only sails ahead faster, a slim, sleek craft cutting through the choppy sea of fellow Amsterdammers. I remember my red beads, still hidden under my collar, and pull them out, my only way of bettering my appearance. By the time we arrive at the Trips, I am almost faint with fear.

Chapter 30

There are two front doors to the Trippenhuis. Magdalena marches to the wide carved door on the left and raps on a panel. "The brother of Johanna's husband lives there," Magdalena explains. She nods to the other door as she straightens her peach silk bodice. "I have met him on several occasions—he is quite a good friend. He calls me 'the Canary' because I am always twittering. Isn't that dear?"

I nod, keeping my face pointed forward. Out of the corner of my eye, I see the fine marble steps of Nicolaes Bruyningh's stoop to my right. If I strain my side vision to the limit, I can see the brass railing of Carel's stoop just beyond.

A stout maid answers the door, wiping her hands on her apron.

"Hallo, Truida," Magdalena says. "It is just I."

The maid glances over her rounded shoulder, revealing

the cap strings that cut into her fleshy neck. "Mevrouw cannot receive visitors now," she says tersely.

Magdalena smiles. "But I am a friend."

The laughter of women comes from somewhere inside.

Magdalena cranes her delicate neck to peer into the house. "Has Johanna company?"

"Mevrouw, if you could please return at—"

"Who is here? I am certain Johanna would want me to enter."

"Mevrouw, please—"

"I recognize that voice! Eva Susanna Pellicorne is here! *She* would want to see me, I am sure."

"Mevrouw—"

Magdalena slips past the maid, who gasps and bustles after her, leaving me standing on the shining marble slab of the doorstep.

Nervously, I toy with my beads. Let Magdalena come out soon. Let us go, before I am seen.

"Cornelia?"

I turn as would a cornered mouse. My knees sag at the sight of Nicolaes Bruyningh, carrying an ebony cane as he walks briskly down the street.

He draws near. "Hallo, Cornelia. I thought that was you, though I could not be sure, as tightly as you hug that door."

I dip my head. "I am waiting for my sister, mijnheer. She visits with the wife of Mijnheer Trip."

"I see." His gaze goes to my beads as he takes off his hat.

After a moment, he lifts his pale blue eyes to mine. "Lovely necklace."

I glance down at it. "It was my moeder's, mijnheer."

He nods. "Coral, isn't it?"

"I think so, mijnheer."

"Do you know the significance of coral to the wearer, my dear?"

I shake my head.

"Coral protects the wearer against evil. No harm can come to the person who wears it. It is quite a powerful charm."

"I did not know, mijnheer."

He taps his cane on a brick. "It is the kind of gift one gives to someone very dear to them."

When will he leave me alone? "My vader gave it to her, I expect."

Stray filaments of gold catch the sunlight as he raises his brows. "Really?"

Just then Magdalena comes rushing out, her pretty face misshapen in a sob. "Come, Cornelia!"

She pushes past Mijnheer Bruyningh. I have but time to give him a quick nod, which he returns with an ice-blue gaze.

"I thought she would be glad to see me," Magdalena says as I run after her. "She didn't have to make me feel like I was barging in. *I* did not know she was having a party. You know my condition—I cannot take upsets like this now."

I glance over my shoulder. Mijnheer Bruyningh is still watching.

"Will you accompany me to my home, Cornelia?" Magdalena asks. "I cannot bear being alone." She frowns at me trailing behind her. "If you do, you may take some refreshment before you go."

"Yes, sister," I say, as if a slice of cheese is sufficient reward for remaining in her company. I take a deep breath. What will Mijnheer Bruyningh report to his brother? That the bastard child of the woman Rembrandt van Rijn would not marry has been lurking about? Yet, he is a nice man, according to Carel. He has made a place for Carel to paint in his attic, and has told Carel, at least Carel says, that he is fond of me. Why would he say such a thing and talk so pleasantly to a nobody like me? It makes no sense.

Magdalena and I speak little more as we make our way down crowded streets. At last we cross the drawbridge over the Singel and duck through the door of the House of the Gilded Scales. "There is cheese in the kitchen," Magdalena says. "Help yourself." She climbs the stairs, hand to her belly. "Titus? Titus, where are you?"

In the kitchen, I cut myself a portion from a yellow wheel of Gouda, and eat it standing next to a spotless marble-topped preparation table. I am gazing at the hanging row of gleaming pots and wondering if Nicolaes Bruyningh will tell Carel that he saw me, when I hear Magdalena scream.

Chapter 31

Titus lies on the four-poster bed, his pale face dwarfed by the fat pillows surrounding him. Though the air coming through the open window is warm and thick, his featherbag is pulled up to his chin.

"Bird," he says when I come in. "I am sorry."

"Shhh! What have you to be sorry for?" I glance in the direction of the door. Downstairs, Magdalena weeps loudly.

He swallows with difficulty. "To worry you and Magdalena."

"I am not worried!" My gaze goes to the pink cherry-sized swelling forming just below his ear.

My scalp tingles with fear.

When he sees me looking, he covers it with his hand. "They just arose."

" 'They'?"

"Bird, they're in my armpits, too."

The burning poison of terror seeps into my gut. "You can have swellings for lots of reasons."

"I saw your moeder die of the plague, Bird. I know what the tokens look like."

I take a shuddering breath. "This is not the plague! It is the sweating sickness. The ague! Something!" I grab the cup of water on the floor next to his bed and put it to his lips. The heat of his skin fires my panic. "Just drink!"

He takes a sip, then falls back. "Help Magdalena, Bird. She's frightened."

I turn away. She is frightened? I am to be brave when the person that is everything to me has the sickness?

I clutch my beads, combing my brain for what I should do. With a start I remember—coral has power.

I fumble to untie the strand. With clumsy hands, I start to tie it around his neck. He moans when I brush the swelling under his ear.

"Sorry!" I pull back, hugging the beads. "This is coral. It protects you from harm. You must wear it."

He squints at the necklace. "Your moeder's red beads?"

How did he know? "Yes. I'll put them on you. I shall be careful."

He shakes his head against the pillow. "They didn't help your moeder."

Tears singe my lids. "Don't say that."

Downstairs, the front door slams.

"WHERE IS MY SON?" Vader roars.

My hands shaking, I hold the beads over him. "You've got to believe, Titus. Let me put them on you."

Vader's steps pound on the stairs. "TITUS! TITUS, LAD!"

I've no time to put them on him. With a glance over my shoulder, I lift the featherbag and dart the beads under Titus's back.

Vader storms into the room. "Son!" He drops down by Titus and grabs his hand. "My son."

I stumble out of the room and wander downstairs, where Neel stands in the hall.

"I came when I heard," he says.

Just seeing the pity in his face makes tears spring to my eyes. "It is nothing," I say hoarsely. "He will be fine. You should go home."

Neel nods, but does not leave.

Four days pass, enough for August to melt into September, though when the mornings end and the evenings begin, I cannot say. We have not been locked in—there are not enough cases in town for the authorities to demand it—yet I have remained at Magdalena's house to minister to Titus. Such a black passage of days. Though I have never lived among such luxury, any pleasure I would have taken in it has become like ashes in my mouth. What do I care for silky sheets, meals taken on china, and the soothing chimes of the golden clock that sits upon the sideboard, when my brother's swellings grow and his strength lessens? Beyond keeping the coral beads tucked safely beneath him, I have tried everything Magdalena's moeder suggests—sponging Titus in vinegar, wrapping him in red flannel, calling the physician to cup his buboes—while Magdalena alternately wails and sleeps in her moeder's arms. Now Vader, stunned by the fear that grips us all, sits like a rock by Titus's bed, as the physician, wearing leather goggles and a beak filled with protective herbs, applies the heated glass to Titus's tokens. Titus hisses in pain. I stumble from the room.

I am downstairs slumped against the wall of the entrance hall when Neel comes from the kitchen with a plate of cheese. He leads me to a chair in the front room, then puts the plate in my lap.

"Eat, Cornelia."

I gaze up at him through a fog of weariness. "Why are you here? Why don't you go home?"

"I cannot rest while"—he looks at me, then away—"my master suffers."

Sighing makes me wince. Even my lungs ache with exhaustion.

"Cornelia, you must eat. What good will it do for you to take sick, too?"

I inch my incredulous gaze up at him. Does he really think I care to live if Titus does not?

"Rest," Neel says. "I will go up with Titus."

I close my eyes and rock my head against the back of the chair. "No. He needs me."

I open my eyes with a thought. "Neel, you said once that your moeder nursed many with the sickness during the last contagion."

His face clouds.

I sit up. "Can you send for her? I know she's in Dordrecht, but I'll—I'll pay. Maybe she knows some treatments we have not tried."

He shakes his head.

"I know I haven't much to offer," I say, "but Magdalena has money—"

"Cornelia, it's not the money."

I sag. "I guess it wasn't fair to ask. It's just that I am—"

"Cornelia, my moeder is dead."

I flinch.

"She died during the contagion," he says gently. "The strain of all the nursing was too much for her." His look is at once tender and sad. "That is why you must eat. I know what can come of exhaustion."

A burning lump swells in my throat. I had chided him once about his happy life at home, and now I find out he has endured great sorrow. Yet, after this and so many slights, he treats me with kindness. I do not deserve it.

"I will not move until you take a bite," Neel says.

I put the cheese to my mouth. It is dust upon my tongue.

Vader glances up from the edge of the bed when I enter, then back down at Titus, who groans softly. Magdalena whimpers as she burrows her face into her moeder's neck while her moeder croons and smoothes her damp brow. Over by the fireplace, the physician strokes the burning sod, then holds the cupping glass to the reddened embers with his tongs. He looks up with his terrible leather beak, a vulture come to feed on my brother, then back into the flames.

He comes away from the fire, bearing the glowing glass before him. "I must cup the buboes on his other side," he says to Vader, his words muffled by the beak. "You must turn him. You, too," he says to me. "Move him slowly, as to not disturb the poisons within him."

I join Vader at the bed, then with a stern nod from the physician, peel back the featherbed and expose Titus's wasted figure. I keep my gaze from the hard, blackened buboes but cannot avoid the raised red spots the size of stuivers covering his pasty flesh. I clench back tears, and steeling myself against the clamminess of his skin and the foul odor of his breath, with Vader I turn him slowly onto his side. Titus coughs, a ringing bark. Magdalena cries out as the physician leans forward with his glass.

Titus opens bloodred eyes. "Bird?"

Vader's icy voice jolts my attention. "What are those?" he growls.

My gaze flashes to Moeder's coral beads, coiled in the dent left in the mattress by Titus's body, then to the impression made by the beads in Titus's flesh. The physician draws back.

"Moeder's beads," I say. Magdalena's moeder watches fearfully, pressing her daughter's face against her shoulder.

"Where did you get them?" Vader demands.

"You. You gave them to me when she died."

"I would have never!" Vader exclaims.

I glance at the physician, his eyes unreadable behind his leather goggles. I lower my voice. "You threw them at me, Vader. When she died."

Vader looks wildly at the physician. "I did not know what I was doing." He rakes his hand through his hair. "Get them away! Now!"

"But they protect him from harm."

"Who told you that drek?"

I cower from the rage building in his face. "Mijnheer Bruyningh—"

"I knew it! I knew I could see it on your face!" He snatches up the necklace, then dashes it to the wall. Beads from the broken strand click on the tile floor.

"Get out," Vader growls. "Run to your Bruyningh. I was a fool to think I could stop you. What are you waiting for? Go!"

"Mijnheer van Rijn!" Magdalena's moeder bleats from her chair, causing Magdalena to sob. "You are deranged!"

I back toward the door. "Go!" he shouts, his voice breaking. "Let me be with my son."

I am running. I am running past peddlers and ladies and dogs. Past gentlemen and horse carts and preachers. Past lepers and dung piles, past nursemaids and children. I am running and running, until at last, with my legs on fire and my head bursting with agony, I am running down the Street That Is the Name of Money.

At the tall house with the many green shutters, I pound on the door.

After an eternity, as I pant and hold my throbbing head, Carel answers.

He takes a step backward. "What are you doing here?" he exclaims.

"Titus is ill!"

His shocked gaze travels up and down my disheveled clothes. "You shouldn't be out."

The words burst from my dry mouth. "He has the tokens upon him."

Carel's eyes widen. He puts his door between us. "Cornelia, what are you thinking?"

I cannot make sense of it. He must not understand. My brother is in trouble.

I step closer. "I've nowhere to go."

Carel wards me off with the door. "Cornelia, please. You need to go home. You're spreading the sickness. You know how I fear it!"

"I—I thought—"

"I'm sorry, Cornelia" He shuts the door.

I take one numb step backward, two, then after a long blank moment, turn, only to find myself stumbling directly into a man's open arms. I cry out before I recognize who it is: Nicolaes Bruyningh.

I smell a whiff of wine as he holds me. "Why, Cornelia, you look like you've seen a ghost."

"You mustn't come near me! The plague is upon Titus and he is dying."

It is only then I feel the full meaning of the words. I hear myself sob.

Mijnheer Bruyningh gathers me to him, enveloping me in his scent of wine and smoke. "Shh, child. Shh."

I push away from him. "No, mijnheer, you mustn't touch me. I've been exposed. Carel has just sent me away."

Mijnheer Bruyningh lets me go but makes no move to distance himself. "The boy's a fool. He does not recognize his own cousin."

Shaking with confusion and sorrow and fear, I swipe at my face with my sleeve. "I don't know what you mean."

He glances over his shoulder, then sighs heavily. "Odd time, odd place, to tell you this. But one does not get to choose the timing of these things, does one? They seem to choose themselves."

He sighs, resigned, as I lift my blurry gaze.

"Come with me, child, you had better step inside."

Chapter 32

I sit in a big chair in Nicolaes Bruyningh's front room, surrounded by heavy wood furniture, blue and white pots filled with spidery plants, and parchment maps on the leather-paneled walls. Blue curls of pipe smoke, scented of overripe cherries, drift by. The air smells of all these things and of a man's spicy flesh—the smell, to my mind, of a rich bachelor's lair. In my shaking hand, a fine china cup rattles against its saucer like chattering teeth.

Nicolaes Bruyningh puffs at his pipe and watches my hand. "You are cold?"

It is the second of September. I would be warm if I were not so numb. I shake my head.

"Do not fear—this tobacco smoke will kill the contagion. You are safe here."

My thin voice is swallowed up by the plushness of the room. "I must get back to Titus."

"Now, now. Drink some tea, it will be good for you."

I watch nervously as he picks up a silver goblet from the carpet-lain table next to him, takes a deep draft, then puts it down. "I had better just come out with it—the quick cut is the less painful." He breathes deeply. "Well, this is it, then: I got Hendrickje with child."

I stare at him in shock, then down at my clinking cup. What does he mean? Had Moeder had another child before me?

"When she first told me, I did not know what to do. I went to my older brother, Jan"—he lowers his head at me—"Carel's vader, as I did for advice in all matters great and small after our own vader died. I was but twenty-two and unsure of myself. As green as new cheese." He sucks on his pipe. "Well, my brother was not pleased, I am sorry to say. He argued that Hendrickje was below us—her vader was but a sergeant in the army, and she, a housemaid to a painter. He said she might very well model naked for his students like a common whore."

I splash warm tea upon my hand, then watch it trickle into my sleeve.

"I assured my brother that Hendrickje would never do such a thing." He studies me, puffing his pipe. "You see, I thought I knew her well. I had spent much of that year, the year Rembrandt painted my portrait, visiting her at Rembrandt's house, and I continued to visit her there almost daily for another two years after that. I told Rembrandt I was interested in his other works in progress." He laughs. "I, who prefer maps to the made-up doodlings of artists!"

I wait as he fills his glass, then takes another pull on his goblet. If he didn't like paintings, why had he asked me for more of my vader's works?

"Well," he says, swallowing his drink, "in all that time, I had never witnessed even a whiff of impropriety on Hendrickje's part. If anything, I thought she kept her distance from her master. They never exchanged so much as a glance in my sight. But my brother was not convinced. He asked me, 'Is this the sort of person with whom you wish to spend your life?' "

I look down at my lap, though through the smoky haze, I can feel Mijnheer Bruyningh's eyes upon me.

"You see, Cornelia, I thought she was. I had given her the coral necklace as a pledge toward our future. You should have seen how happy that made her, just a simple coral necklace. I might as well have given her a shipload of jewels. I can still see her sweet face glowing as I tied it around her neck. We were in Rembrandt's courtyard." He sighs. "Pink roses were blooming on the trellis. I picked her one, to go along with the necklace, and tucked it behind her ear. From then on, pink roses were our flower. I see she planted one in the courtyard when she moved to the Rozengracht—your house." He brings his glass to his lips. "Her happiness gave me such pleasure."

As he drinks, I turn toward the sound of a child's laughter outside the open window. How I wish to escape! But he speaks again, his words pinning me to my seat like a spider binding a moth in its web.

"My brother's attitude confused me," he says. "Weeks earlier, I had brought Hendrickje home for him to meet. I had felt sure he would see my reasons for loving her. He'd been cool to her then, but to be cool was his way, so I thought little of it. I thought he'd come around. So when I told him of Hendrickje's news—of *our* news—I expected his blessing. Instead—" He draws a breath, then purses his lips. "He was very harsh."

His brother is Carel's vader. The same man who forced Carel to give up painting . . . and me. I shudder.

"I was stung into inaction. For three long weeks, I did not go to her. My brother said, 'You gave her a gift, didn't you? The little necklace? Let her keep it. You owe her nothing.' When I told him she would be crushed, he said, 'Better a disappointment now than years of unhappiness trying to fit into Kloveniersburgwal society.' He said I knew as well as he that a sergeant's daughter would never be accepted.

"Then I asked him, 'What about our child?'" He lifts his goblet, pausing before he drinks. "He said, 'Maybe it will die.'"

I put my cup on the table, hating him and his brother for treating my moeder this way. What did Moeder do with the baby? Why did she never tell me of it? Have I another big brother or sister in the world? And then I remember Titus. I start to rise. "I must go."

"Sit," says Nicolaes Bruyningh.

I shrink back.

"Hear me out. I was wrong, Cornelia. It took me three long weeks to figure it out, but finally, I came to my senses.

That Saturday morning when I woke up, it was as clear to me as an Antwerp diamond: no matter what my brother thought, I wanted Hendrickje. I wanted our child.

"I rushed out of the house, my brother shouting after me. When I got to Rembrandt's, I checked the courtyard. No Hendrickje. I checked the kitchen. No Hendrickje. I bounded up the stairs to ask Rembrandt if he might know where she was. I threw open the studio door." He draws a breath, then lets it out slowly. "She was sitting before him, naked, my beads wrapped in her hair."

I bow my head. It is a long time before I lift it, but when I do, he is puffing on his pipe, waiting behind his veil of smoke.

"You know the painting of which I speak, don't you?" he says quietly. "I can see it in your eyes."

"The picture in the attic," I whisper.

"I see. Is it still there?"

I cannot swallow the lump that chokes me. So this is the picture he was seeking when he asked to buy one of Vader's older "biblical" works. Does he really think I would give it to him and expose Moeder in this way?

"Has anyone seen it?" he asks. "I suppose he could pass it for a depiction of Bathsheba going to King David's bed, make a few guilders from it. God knows Rembrandt needs them."

Suddenly, I remember Neel mentioning Vader's painting of Bathsheba. He has seen the picture. But would he have recognized the model? "I do not think so," I murmur, sick with humiliation.

"I would not want your moeder seen that way."

I frown in fierce agreement, though even after seeing my moeder shamed, Neel has not spoken out against her.

Bruyningh rests his head in his hand, pushing his graying yellow curls from his ruddy face. "After I saw her with Rembrandt like that, I ran off. And I did not go back—not for several years. I thought she was his then. Or at least that she was not the girl I thought she was." He looks up. "You do understand, don't you, Cornelia?"

Why did Moeder do it? Why did she choose Vader over Bruyningh, and model for Vader in the worst possible way? And more importantly—what became of the baby?

Nicolaes Bruyningh smiles with one side of his mouth. "In the years after that, my brother tried to make matches for me. A rich young widow from Haarlem. An alderman's sister who lived on the Prinzengracht. Johanna de Geer's comely niece. But I couldn't marry, Cornelia, not even if it was the Stadholder's own daughter." He shakes his head as if wet. "So I threw myself into business. Helped Jan raise his children. Went to sea and did some things that I wasn't proud of."

He drinks long from his goblet, then wipes his mouth. "But I loved your mother, Cornelia; I couldn't get her out of my head. And truth be known, I loved our child, too."

I can stand it no longer. "Then where is it?"

He levels his gaze at me. "Oh, my dear, I thought you understood. The child is you."

Chapter 33

Through rotted-cherry tendrils of pipe smoke, I look at my soap-chapped hands, now clenched on my lap. These are Bruyningh hands. A rich man's blood runs through them. Ship-owning blood. Who is this girl called Cornelia? She is a stranger to me.

I hear the glug of wine as Nicolaes Bruyningh refills his goblet. "Do you not remember seeing me as a little one?" he asks as he pours. "I would walk by your house, just to get a glimpse of you."

An image fights its way into the turmoil in my brain. I see the Gold Mustache Man, pushing back his hat to listen to me, the bristly gold hair of his mustache shining in the sun. My heart swells. How I wanted him to be my friend, to be my vader. The being inside me had yearned for him, blood calling out to blood, knowing something that I did not.

Now the image of the younger Gold Mustache Man dissolves into the present Nicolaes Bruyningh, clean shaven, hard faced, and with his head cocked as if listening for my thoughts. He smiles as if he hears them. "You liked the doll, didn't you?"

Even as I picture my precious ivory-faced doll, my mind wanders to another place. I am feeling the rain soaking my hair and beads pressing into my palm as my insides roil in misery. I see the Gold Mustache Man, slipping on the bricks, running away.

"You ran," I say.

He takes another swallow of wine. "Hardly admirable, I admit. It was the shock. I was coming to claim my woman and my child. As you see, my timing has always been execrable."

My heart pounds as I look at the hardened but handsome man in the velvet doublet, sitting in his leather chair, the smoke of his pipe curling from his hand. My vader, Nicolaes Bruyningh.

All these years I have suffered without him. I should have never had to worry about my next meal. I should have never had to wear rags. I should have never been burdened with the shame of being a crazy man's bastard. I catch my breath. But now I'm this man's bastard. Moeder had not married him, either. What does it matter whose bastard I am? I will always bear the shame of not belonging.

Nicolaes Bruyningh sucks on his pipe. "I couldn't believe it when I heard of you from Carel. God will have his jest! My nephew was falling in love with his own first cousin, and he did not even know it. And then I thought—of course. Cousins can marry. They do it all the time to keep wealth within a family. Why not bring you into our fold, not for the money, of course, but for my own satisfaction? God knows I've paid for it."

He takes a small sip. "Ironic, isn't it? Through Jan's own son you will enter into the family." He half smiles. "Jan will get over it. He will have to, now."

My heartbeat quickens. Carel had shut the door in my face. Even if he had his family's blessing to wed me, would he want to? Think of it if he did: a handsome husband—a fine house—ships!—all mine. Me—a Bruyningh two times over, through blood and marriage. I would never be in want again.

"Look at your reflection in that mirror." Mijnheer Bruyningh points with his pipe to a round mirror in a gilt frame hanging on the leather-paneled wall. "Oh, I know your coloring is different—there you are your moeder's daughter—but have you honestly never noticed? That is not van Rijn's small eyes or pudgy nose—you have my features, the Bruyningh nose. Carel's got it, too."

I lean toward the mirror and frown at the image that has given me so much dissatisfaction over the years. There, under my cap, is my moeder's red-brown hair, which is given to waves. There are her large brown eyes.

I glance nervously back at Nicolaes Bruyningh, who holds

his face still as if daring me to compare it to mine, then return my gaze to the mirror.

Before my frightened eyes, something strange begins to happen. Up onto the cheekbones I had thought all these years to be like Moeder's, wells the imprint of Bruyningh's own bones. My eyes, though brown, begin to bear the unmistakable stamp of Bruyningh's. Even my nose reveals itself to be a small, neat copy of his. It is as if empowered by the truth, the thing that has lain coiled quietly inside me all these years has crept silently to the surface.

Bruyningh laughs at my expression. "You see? You cannot deny it—you've Bruyningh written all over you. How it must have tortured your—" He frowns slightly. "—Rembrandt."

I swing my horrified gaze back to Bruyningh. "He knows?"

"If Hendrickje tried to keep it a secret, it wouldn't have lasted long after you were born, not with that face. But that wouldn't be like Hendrickje. She was too honest. She would have told him." He sucks on his pipe. "I hope it burned his soul."

Memories of Vader shunning me in his studio, of giving away my doll, of never painting me, tumble through my brain. How he must have hated the sight of me, another man's child, another mouth to feed when he could hardly feed his own. Why did he not turn me out, me and Moeder both? Why did he not let us go to Bruyningh? We could have been rich. He could have had his memories of his dear Saskia and Titus all to himself.

Titus.

I jump up. "I must go."

"Where, my dear?"

"To Titus. I've been gone too long."

His cool fingers brush my arm when he reaches out to me. "Is that wise, my dear? You could become ill yourself."

I shudder, thinking of Carel shutting the door on me upon hearing of Titus's distemper. To save his skin, he turned me away in my hour of need. But I can't think of that now. I must help Titus.

I look toward the door. "I really must go. He's so very ill. I can—I can come back."

"No. What can you do for him? You're not a physician. Let me send a servant around, make inquiries as to his progress. It's safer that way."

"But what about the servant?"

He frowns, puzzled. "What about him?"

"He could catch the contagion."

He shrugs. "He's but a servant. What do we care? Now, now, don't pull that look. He's a sturdy enough sort. He will be fine."

I remember Carel mentioning the loss of thousands of slaves as if they were just another cargo. Slaves, servants, *my moeder*—whomever the Bruyninghs deemed inferior mattered less than little to them. Then I think of Vader, with his respect for the man with the pearl-gray eyes; for Mijnheer Gootman, the cobbler whom he painted as a king; for a woman carrying a child that wasn't even his. Moeder. My heart goes out to him—and then I remember he has thrown me out, too.

I take a painful breath. I cannot sort this out now. Titus needs me.

I start toward the door.

Nicolaes Bruyningh puts down his cup and stands up to block me. "Titus is not even your blood, Cornelia. Why are you risking your life for him, when you can stay here safe with me?"

How can he ask? The reason is so clear. "Because he loves me. And because I love him."

He lays his hand to my wrist with fingers hard as stone. "As your vader, I am afraid I cannot stand for this foolish reasoning."

I draw back. "For going to my brother?"

"For fighting for a lost cause."

I stare at his hand, then up at his face. What gives him the right to stop me now when he abandoned me all these years? "You never came for me."

"I couldn't. Did you want me to lose everything? What good would I be to you without my money?"

I try to picture myself as his well-dressed daughter, living in luxury, drowning in guilders.

"We can start fresh, Cornelia. You've been given this chance. Take it."

I see the face of my dear brother, his jaw clenched in quiet agony, and of Vader, unshaven and frightened, fretting over him and growling to his God. Blood kin or not, for richer or poorer, through bad times and good, I find that I love Rembrandt van Rijn in spite of all of his imperfections. Perhaps, I think with wonder, because of his imperfections. I pull my arm free.

My footsteps ring from the polished tiles as I run. "Do you know what you are doing?" he shouts after me.

I do not, not entirely, as I wrestle open the door. But of one thing I am certain: Though I may have the Bruyningh blood, I do not have the Bruyningh heart.

Chapter 34

Vader is sponging Titus's brow when I return to the House of the Gilded Scales. Though it has been but an hour or two, it seems as if time has stopped. Perhaps it has, between Vader and me. I stare at him as he tenderly ministers to Titus, touching his son's brow as if it could break, and wait for him to shout me out of the house.

Vader frowns when he sees me watching. "You're back," he says in his guttural growl.

I go to my brother, expecting Vader's protests. I can feel Titus's heat when I lean over him. He does not open his eyes.

I swallow back the burning coal that chokes me. "Where is the physician?" I whisper hoarsely to Vader.

"Gone." Vader looks down at his son, then lovingly touches his cheek. "He sleeps now like a baby."

My chest is painfully tight. "Where is Magdalena?"

"She and her moeder have left for relatives in St. Annaparochie."

How like Magdalena to think only of herself when her husband is in such danger! "How can she leave him like this?" I cry, expecting Vader to rebuke both Magdalena and me.

Vader shakes his head. "Do not judge her ill. She is with child. It was the right thing to do."

"Right thing." I kick my heel against the floor. So he does not throw me out. Yet. Maybe I wish he would.

Vader turns to look at me, then draws in a breath. "What is the matter, Cornelia?"

I break free from his gaze and glance at Titus. "Not now, not with Titus—"

"He's exhausted. He will sleep." Vader sinks wearily onto a stool, the sponge still in his hand. "So out with it. You have the look of a cat ready to pounce."

I straighten myself. All these years he let me live a lie. I try to swallow but my mouth has gone dry. "I know who my real vader is."

He inhales sharply, then slowly lets it out. "So you talked to Bruyningh."

"Yes."

He sighs heavily. "Did he tell you everything?"

"Yes."

"Then you shall hear everything from me as well." He dumps the sponge on the table next to him. "I wonder how well our stories will match."

"Go ahead," I say grimly.

He rakes his fingers through his sparse hair, leaving it sticking up. "I don't know where to start."

"What about the picture?" I demand.

"What picture?"

"The one in our attic. Of Moeder in her . . . nakedness."

"Oh. That one." He touches Titus's cheek.

"Why did you make Moeder model naked for it?" I whisper harshly. "She didn't model before then. He said so."

Vader sits up sharply. "Nicolaes Bruyningh" he snarls, pronouncing the name as if it were poison, "does not know everything that goes on around here. But yes, he is right. She did not model naked for me before then. Nor did she after."

"So why did you make her? Did you not know that if anyone ever saw the picture she would be reviled?"

"I never intended for anyone to see it."

"Then why would you paint it?"

"It was an act of love."

"An act of love!"

"Yes, if you can believe that."

"I don't know what to believe anymore."

He smiles bitterly. "You have no idea how much I loved your mother."

"You had some fine way of showing it."

"I ask you to listen."

I fold my arms and wait.

He shakes his head. "You don't know. From the moment

she stepped foot in the house as a sixteen-year-old, I was drawn to her."

"You were an old man!"

"Don't you think I knew that? A ridiculous old widower. I kept my distance from her. Still, I couldn't keep my mind from her. Just being in the same room with her made me giddy. When I wasn't painting, when I *was* painting, she was all I could think about."

I think of my yearnings for Carel, how such an attraction can drive all sense from one's head. But this is not about Carel and me. "Why did you not just marry her, then? It was because she was your maid, wasn't it?"

"That did not help matters, but no, it wasn't because she was my maid. I was still getting over my loss of Saskia, and Hendrickje was twenty years my junior—I felt repulsive to her. So I kept my distance. I hardly spoke to the girl."

This rings true. Nicolas Bruyningh had said there had been no improprieties.

"Then why didn't you just let Nicolaes Bruyningh have her?" I demand. "He was more her age. He was rich, too."

"Bruyningh. I didn't like him chasing after Hendrickje, but I let him have his chance. Looked the other way for three whole years. Gad, the boy was slow."

Titus stirs. I take up the sponge and wipe his face with it. "Titus?" I whisper.

He does not open his eyes. I lay my hand on his burning cheek.

"Bruyningh was not so slow, however," Vader says, his lips curled with disgust, "that he did not eventually get her with child."

I glare at Vader as I sponge Titus. "You knew this when you painted her?" I whisper angrily. "How could you have taken advantage of her like that?"

"Just listen, would you? I'd seen her crying. So I asked what was wrong. When she told me the cad had left her in a state, I told her I would take care of her." A young man's fire smolders in Vader's watery eyes. "I wanted to kill him."

I cannot keep the bitterness from my voice. "So you take care of her by making her model naked."

"You make it sound evil, but it was not. When she turned to me in her grief, I could no longer hide my feelings. I was ready to shout from every bridge in town of my love for Hendrickje Stoffels. I promised her I'd care for her . . ." He gazes at me with a tenderness that confuses me. "And you."

"If you loved her so much, why did you not marry her then? Make me your legal child? Did you not think how much not doing so would hurt me?"

"I haven't finished telling the story! I was going to marry her. We planned to publish our first banns that Sunday. I was so in love, Cornelia. I wanted to breathe your moeder in, meld her soul to mine—oh, she was a wondrous girl!" He closes his eyes, his old man's face wreathed in a smile.

He opens his eyes. "It was her idea for me to paint her. Her gift to me, and mine to her. A sacred act. She knew how much I worshipped her, and she loved my painting. Back then, like you, she seemed to understand it. So that Saturday morning, a day I had no pupils, and after Titus left for his uncle's, I shut the studio door behind us and bade her to sit. She placed herself upon a drape and, turning her head away, gave up her body to my artist's brush.

"I had prepared the background in advance, so I was able to begin painting her figure at once. The work went quickly, spurred by both passion and the tenderness of her sacrifice. Do not judge me—I am speaking the truth about the woman I loved! The moment I laid brush to canvas I knew it would be a masterpiece, yet I planned to never show a soul. It was between her and me. All morning long I painted in our private ecstasy, until—he burst in."

"Nicolaes Bruyningh."

"I'm sick of that name! Yes. It was an ugly scene. He shouted at Hendrickje. She wrapped herself in a drape and cried. I threatened him with a paint trowel. He went away, but not before he shattered Hendrickje's world with a threat."

We stare at each other.

"What?" I ask.

"He said he was taking away his child because its mother was a whore. He said the courts would be on his side—the picture would be his proof."

"He was taking me?"

"I told him I would destroy the painting. He said it did not matter, the Bruyninghs had the power to sway the judges, and mark his words, he would do it. He would take away his child. And then he left."

"But he said he would take me?"

"Yes. But not your moeder. It would have killed her."

"Why did you not marry her then, make your own claim and become my legal vader? It was Saskia's will that stopped you, wasn't it? You would have lost Saskia's money if you married."

He blew air between his lips. "I could have cared less about the money! I thought I could always make more of it painting. I'd been successful before; I thought the wheel would turn back for me. No, it was Hendrickje's wish that we did not marry. She didn't want to do anything to inflame Bruyningh into taking you."

"She didn't marry you . . . because of me?"

He shakes his head slowly. "She didn't want to lose you, Cornelia. Neither of us did."

I bow my head, unable to comprehend.

"What that woman had to endure," Vader says. "She was called to the church court three times and made to confess her sin of living with me outside of marriage. My patrons treated her like dirt. 'The painter's whore,' they called her. How they smirked. I lost all my wealthiest patrons, but I didn't care. Not if they insulted her."

"Why didn't he—?"

"Take you? I don't know. We saw him roaming by our

house. The threat was always there. I think he was holding out hope that she would return to him."

I open my mouth, then shut it. He wasn't holding out hope. He would have never risked being cut off from his money. If he couldn't be happy, he wanted to be certain my moeder wasn't, either.

Vader rubs his forehead. "Later, much later, by memory, I finished her face in the picture. I painted the look of resignation she had worn the day he'd left. Her sadness burned itself on my soul. It haunts me still. I think, Cornelia, that she loved your vader more than me."

I draw in a breath as if stung. My vader. Who is my vader? Bruyningh, the man who gave me life? Or Rembrandt, the one with whom I'd lived it?

There is a light knock on the door frame. Vader looks up.

Neel stands in the doorway, his hat in his hands. "How does he fare, mijnheer?"

I gaze at Neel's face. His true concern for Titus, for our family, is writ all over it. All these months I have turned him away, ignoring his friendship, while pining for a boy who shut me out when he heard my brother was ill. How could I not see what a treasure Neel's goodness and honesty have been? But it is too late for me to tell him this, to ask for his friendship. The best I can do is to lessen his chances of getting ill.

"Neel, please, you must go," I say. "You will get the contagion."

His face, always an open book, becomes a study of hurt

and concern. "But I have been with him, same as you. If I have got the sickness, it is already upon me. Why will you not take my help when you so need it?"

Next to me, Vader gets up wearily, an old soldier rising to yet another battle. "Let him help, Cornelia. Don't you know? God protects saints and madmen." He smiles sadly. "Perhaps they are the same."

Chapter 35

The groans of the four ragged men manning the ropes are lost in the sounds of the city around us. Over the cries of peddlers and the clopping of horses, I barely hear the thud of the wooden casket bumping against the dirt walls as it is lowered into the grave. There is a final thud, one last murmured prayer. The preacher turns to shake our hands, just Vader, me, and Neel. No one comes to the funeral of a plague victim, not even, it seems—as Magdalena remains with her kin—one's wife.

Now Vader and I trudge through the Westermarkt, having parted with Neel in front of the church. Even with Vader at my side, I am completely alone; the everyday sounds of people shopping and selling exist in a separate sphere. They have nothing to do with me. It is as if I have died with Titus. If only I had.

"Do you hear them?" Vader says.

I fight my way through invisible walls of sorrow to look at him. I notice his cheeks and chin are bristly with stubble—I'd not thought to shave him since Titus fell ill. Ah, well, what does it matter now.

"The bells," Vader says.

I close my eyes, willing myself to go back into the world around us, if only for a moment. I hear the death bells of the Westerkerk.

"The bells must be for Titus," Vader says wonderingly. "Though I don't know how."

They cannot be for Titus. Vader has no loose stuivers, not even for Titus's grave. Magdalena's family had to rent it. They say later they will move the body to their tomb in the church, when the plague has passed.

My gut tightens. Could Nicolaes Bruyningh have paid for them? Could he have heard about Titus's death and made this gesture of claim upon me?

Vader plods on, the bells tolling, tolling behind us. I move to catch up, when I think, He is not blood. With Titus gone, Rembrandt and I have no connection. Will he want me to remain? Do I want to remain with him?

I gasp when Neel jogs up behind me. Vader moves on as I stop to catch my breath now that even breathing is a chore.

"Sorry to frighten you," Neel says, his plain face drawn with concern. "May I accompany you home?"

I gaze at him, the bells still bellowing overhead. "I don't know where home is."

His expression is so full of pity and sorrow that it makes me almost laugh in spite of my misery. *Oh, Neel. You are the true Worry Bird. I know, now, I would cherish even the slenderest of friendships with you, should I remain in Rembrandt's house.*

Rembrandt is already shut up in his studio when we arrive at the house on the Rozengracht. I go to the kitchen though I don't know what to do there. The stacks of dirty pots, the pile of soiled linen—all look strange. I hear Neel upstairs, knocking on the studio door.

"Mijnheer? May I come in?"

I look out the kitchen window to the courtyard, where the rose vine climbs, fragrant in its second bloom. The roses Moeder planted for Nicolaes Bruyningh. Had she ever stopped loving him? I shall never know.

The death bells stop. Over on their step, the van Roop girls play with dolls. The youngest one hugs her doll to her chest and rocks it back and forth. When I turn away from the window, I hear Neel's muffled voice upstairs. I am so overcome by loneliness that I trudge upstairs to join them.

"Please, mijnheer," Neel says as I enter the studio. "You must paint. That will be your cure."

Vader sags on his stool, his hands in his lap. "I just do not feel like it."

Neel nods, then turns his hand to grinding a chunk of pigment. I sink onto the stool next to Vader's abandoned canvas of Tenderest Love. Six days of watching Titus slip away has left me as empty as a bell. I rest, thinking of nothing in particular, until I begin to notice the scraping sound of Neel's paint trowel as he mixes the light ochre pigment with linseed oil. I hear the cooing of doves on the windowsill. The ridiculous tootling of the organ in the New Maze Park. Tijger strolls in, climbs onto a pile of canvas, and begins to take a bath, his tongue lapping noisily.

Neel glances from Vader to me, then loads a dab of yellow onto his palette. He mixes some of it with other small dabs he has placed beside it, then lifts a canvas to an empty easel. It is the picture of the Prodigal Son.

The painting has been worked on since I noticed it last. Most of the figures have been fleshed out, especially the vader and the son. Neel once said he painted *The Prodigal Son* because he was interested in forgiveness, in its healing power. If only forgiveness could heal wounds like mine. If only simple forgiveness could make me know who I am and what I should be.

Now Neel adds a stroke to the picture, to the hands the vader has placed on his kneeling son's shoulders. He adds another one, then stands back. "I cannot get it, mijnheer. It needs your eye."

Vader gets up with a heavy sigh. With dragging steps, he comes to Neel's side and wordlessly takes the brush. Silent tears flow down his bristly cheeks as he paints the penitent kneeler.

Suddenly, he stops. He gives Neel the brush. "I cannot do this anymore."

"Mijnheer."

"My art—what good has come from it? All my time, all my love, everything I have poured into it while my dear ones pass through their lives. Then they're gone, and I have nothing. Nothing."

I turn away from the sounds of whirring duck wings as they land upon the canal. "Vader," I say, surprising even myself. "What about me? Will you care when I am gone?"

Neel puts down his palette and comes to me. He puts a protective hand to my shoulder, then bends over me. "Shh, Cornelia," he whispers in my ear. "Do you not know? He values you above all else, but he does not know how to tell you. He's a man of paint, not words."

A lump swells in my throat. Could it be true? Could Rembrandt really love me? Could he think of me as his own, even though I am not? Even though I am Bruyningh's? I glance away with stinging eyes. Neel squeezes my hand.

Vader looks up. He gazes sadly at us. Then, suddenly, his eyes widen.

"Vader? What is wrong?"

"Cornelia! Oh! Be still. Neel, please do not move."

Neel and I exchange puzzled glances.

"No! No! As you were!" Vader rushes to the canvas of Tenderest Love with his palette. "Thank you, God," he whispers, "thank you." He sketches an outline in black paint, his eyes wild.

There is a knock at the door downstairs.

I move to get it.

"No!" Vader cries. He shouts toward the open window, "Come upstairs! We're busy!"

Is it Carel at the door? Nicolaes? To my surprise I find myself dreading both. I cannot be a part of their world of ships and power and selfishness. I do not want to be. I look at Vader painting, his sleeve jangling with energy as he works. A sudden surge of pride in him, in his work, in his unfathomable friendship with God, tells me all I need to know though I've been too stubborn to see it: I have paint running through my veins. I am Rembrandt's daughter, even if he never acknowledges me.

Slow footsteps sound on the risers. At last someone appears at the door. A small boy.

He draws back from the three intense stares boring into him.

Neel lets out a breath as if relieved. I glance at him, wondering who he thought the visitor might be.

"Oh," he says. "Hello, lad. You came from the church."

"Please, mijnheer," the boy says to him. He holds out a little pouch. "You gave us too much."

Neel frowns.

"For the bells, mijnheer."

"Keep it for yourself," Neel says. He glances at me. I stare back. He paid for the bells?

The boy's eyes grow large. "Really?"

I gape, not only at the boy, but at the outrageousness of it all: Neel cares for me, for my vader, and he is still here in spite of my foolishness.

"Cornelia," Vader barks, "you have completely lost your expression!"

Neel waves the boy to scoot.

"Thank you, mijnheer!" The boy clatters down the stairs.

Slowly, as if fearful of what he does, Neel slides me a small, tender smile. For the merest moment, I smile shyly in return. I glance away, wondering at such sweetness in such a time of sorrow.

"Oh," Vader cries, "that is perfect. Perfect! Hold it! Cornelia, girl, what would I do without you?"

And then, for one breathless moment, my eyes meet Vader's. Before I can ponder it, before I can resist, something swims up from the depths of each of us, and sliding along a slender tendril of hope, touches.

"Brilliant," Vader whispers, and then the moment is gone.

For many hours after that, I hold my pose. His sleeve wagging, Vader paints onto his canvas, his strokes slowly becoming my face, the face of his daughter. And Neel, my good Neel, holds my hand, steadying me for my journey ahead.

Chapter 36

The small, plump man shakes me from my reverie with his peevish voice. "We have looked around, young lady, and we'd like to make a few offers. Could you relay them to your agent?"

I look out onto the murky green water of the canal, where a pair of ducks drift, their ducklings darting after them. Godspeed, friends. I close the window and catch the lock. "Relay the offers to me, please. I am in charge here."

Big Baby puffs his lips in indecision. "I suppose she could be," he says as if I am out of hearing. "I did hear that Rembrandt has no survivors. His son and his son's wife died, all in the space of a year."

At least the Stork has the good sense to know that they might be offensive. He turns away his lanky form to whisper, "I think there might have been another daughter. By his—"

They turn and look at me.

They have no power to hurt me now—we are going to a new land, where we can start out fresh. "What items are you interested in?" I ask.

Big Baby holds up a tall framed picture.

I wince. He would pick that one.

"I'm sorry, that's not for sale." Neel comes across the room and kisses my cheek. Even though we have been wed for nearly three weeks, the feel of it still thrills me. "Sorry, gentlemen," he says. "I am keeping that one. It has special significance to me."

When Big Baby continues to hold on to it as if in defiance, Neel walks over and gently prizes it out of his hand. "I'm sorry, mijnheer, but it was a new artist's first painting. It will be valuable someday. You understand, don't you?"

Big Baby crosses his arms and begins to make a fuss, but Neel pats him on the back and escorts him to the door. "You still need to pack your books, Cornelia," Neel says over his shoulder. The Stork puts down the old helmet with a last longing look and follows.

As Neel ushers them to the stairway, I place the painting he has saved next to the canvas my vader painted of Tenderest Love and stand back to judge it. The painting of the crane is not one of technical genius, but I am learning. I am learning.

Acknowledgments

I wish to thank good friends/excellent writers Barbara Timberlake Russell and Nancy Butts for their suggestions and encouragement during the early stages of writing *I Am Rembrandt's Daughter*. To my friend and legendary librarian Ruth Berberich, my daughter and judicious critic Lauren Cullen, and my publicity guru and fellow dreamer Brandy Nagel, I also owe many thanks for their readings and wise comments on subsequent revisions. A special thanks goes to Elizabeth Barten for her reading of the manuscript with an eye for things Dutch. I must thank, too, my daughters Alison and Megan for their support for a project that has taken so long to develop it must seem like family to them.

Finally, I'd like to heartily thank my literary agent, Barbara Kouts, for cheering me on from the beginning, Deb Shapiro, for making publicity work fun, and Melanie Cecka, my smart and insightful editor, to whom I will always be grateful for her part in bringing to light a story that is so very close to my heart.

I Am Rembrandt's Daughter is a work of fiction, and therefore I have on occasion taken liberties with the historical record when it suited my story. On the whole, though, I tried to stick as closely to the facts as possible, and so good research material was essential. I would therefore like to acknowledge the following authors on whose works I based my tale: Simon Schama (*Rembrandt's Eyes*, Alfred A. Knopf, 1999); Gary Schwartz (*Rembrandt: His Life, His Paintings*, Viking, 1985); Ernst Van de Wetering (*Rembrandt: The Painter at Work*, University of California Press, Berkeley, 2000); and Paul Zumthor (*Daily Life in Rembrandt's Holland*, Stanford University Press, 1994).

Author's Note

I Am Rembrandt's Daughter is a fictional story that sprang from my personal interpretations of Rembrandt and his work and my research into Amsterdam in the Golden Age. As I became acquainted with Rembrandt's world, two paintings particularly intrigued me: *Bathsheba with King David's Letter*—a painting of his common-law wife, Hendrickje Stoffels—and his portrait of Nicolaes Bruyningh. I wondered why Hendrickje looked so heartbreakingly regretful in the Bathsheba painting. And who was this charming young man with the wistful smile, this adorable Nicolaes Bruyningh? I was half in love just looking at him.

Hendrickje had come to work for Rembrandt in 1649, while Bruyningh's portrait was painted in 1652. The two young people would have been in contact . . . but could there have been more to their story? Only after I knew Rembrandt could I figure out how the lives of Hendrickje, Nicolaes, Rembrandt, and his daughter, Cornelia, might have intersected.

Rembrandt van Rijn was born on July 15, 1606, the eighth of nine children, to a miller and his wife. He must have seemed especially bright to his parents because he was the only of their children they enrolled in higher education. It was soon clear that the fourteen-year-old Rembrandt's heart was in painting, and he was sent to study first for three years under Jacob Isaacsz van Swanenburgh and then with Pieter Lastman, the most successful painter in Rembrandt's hometown of Leiden. Within six months Rembrandt was more advanced than his teacher, and he and another talented student, Jan Lievens, set off for the bright lights of Amsterdam to find their fortune.

And find it they did. Within months people in the highest circles in Amsterdam were talking about these two "beardless youths," and aristocrats lined up at the door of the miller's son for their portraits. Rembrandt became a master at etching, too, eventually selling prints at the then unheard of price of one hundred guilders each. He did so well that he was able to woo and eventually marry the respectable, modestly wealthy Saskia van Uylenburgh in 1634. Saskia was a cousin of Rembrandt's art dealer, Hendrick van Uylenburgh. To celebrate his newfound wealth and prestige, Rembrandt bought a mansion on the Breestraat, where he set up a workshop that attracted top students like Ferdinand Bol, Gerard Dou, Nicolaes

Maes, Samuel van Hoogstraten, and Govert Flinck—painters who would go on to have their own illustrious careers.

But Rembrandt quickly found himself chafing under the restrictions of the popular tastes of the time. He experimented with composition in his group portraits and history paintings, arranging figures to tell a dramatic story, instead of just lining people up in an unimaginative way. He played with the effect of lighting, using a technique called *chiaroscuro*, as Cornelia points out in our story. His experimentation in composition and lighting resulted in what is now considered his most famous painting, *The Night Watch*, a wildly dramatic picture of a company of volunteer soldiers.

Modern legend has it that *The Night Watch* outraged Rembrandt's contemporaries and began his slide into shame and poverty. Though it is true that his style contributed to his financial ruin—he was piling on his paint thickly when the popular fashion was for highly polished work with invisible strokes—it was his controversial personal life that would cause his fall from favor.

While Rembrandt was working on *The Night Watch*, his wife, Saskia, died, leaving him a heartbroken widower with a one-year-old son, Titus. Rembrandt soon had a romantic affair with Titus's nurse, Geertje Dircx. Although scandalous, the relationship didn't initially cause his patrons to turn away. Things began to sour when Rembrandt sent a very loudly and publicly protesting Geertje to a women's jail after she wouldn't leave him alone. Rembrandt then took up with a young maidservant in the household, Hendrickje Stoffels, further damaging his image. Not only did Rembrandt not hide the fact that he was in love with this daughter of a common army sergeant, he welcomed the daughter she bore him out of wedlock in October 1654—Cornelia.

Hendrickje appeared before church elders to be reprimanded for bearing a child outside of marriage. Meanwhile, Rembrandt's wealthy friends and patrons, already shocked by his treatment of Geertje Dircx and by his squandering of money, stopped associating with him. Rembrandt ignored them, and they stopped buying his work. It's not clear why Rembrandt wouldn't marry Hendrickje; he left no letters or documents recording his thoughts. True, Saskia's will had stipulated that Rembrandt would lose the money she'd left him if he ever remarried, but Rembrandt always believed he would sell more paintings and wouldn't need Saskia's money.

So why didn't he marry Hendrickje? When looking around for reasons, I lit upon my favorite portrait of Nicolaes Bruyningh, who died a wealthy bachelor in 1680, leaving among his worldly goods Rembrandt's portrait of him wearing a wistful smile. Why didn't *he* marry? And what of the mysterious girl called Cornelia, about whom so little is known? This is where my imagination came in. I created Carel Bruyningh, one of the few fictitious characters in the book, to connect Cornelia and Nicolaes—and a story was born.

Though he remained famous his entire life, Rembrandt never did reclaim the popularity of his youth. He went bankrupt and lost the big house on the Breestraat in 1658, and was forced to move to a workingman's part of town, the Jordaan, directly across the street from an amusement park called the New Maze. This didn't stop him from creating his best work. The ability of this difficult man to portray the inner workings of the human heart shines in the painting now known as *The Jewish Bride*, the work I have Rembrandt refer to as "Tenderest Love" at the end of *I Am Rembrandt's Daughter*. Upon seeing this painting in 1885, Vincent van Gogh said, 'I should be happy to give ten years of my life if I could go on sitting here in front of this picture for a fortnight, with only a crust of dry bread for food.' That such a flawed man as Rembrandt could paint such beauty is, to me, truly something to ponder. Genius, evidently, is not reserved for the perfect.

Rembrandt died of unknown causes on October 4, 1669, a year after Titus's death. He was sixty-three years old. Two weeks after Rembrandt's death, Titus's wife, Magdalena van Loo succumbed to the plague. Titus and Magdalena's eleven-month-old daughter, Titia, was spared, and lived in Amsterdam to the age of forty-six. Due to overcrowding in the van Loo family tomb, Titus's body was never moved within the church. Like his father, he lies in an unmarked grave in the Westerkerk.

Where did this leave Cornelia? Though not yet sixteen, she wed painter Cornelis Suythof ("Neel") less than a year after Rembrandt died, in May 1670. She and Cornelis then moved to Batavia in the Dutch East Indies, where Cornelis took the position as jail keeper to supplement his income as a painter. Whether or not Cornelia attempted to paint is not known, though I like to think she might have, surrounded as she was by art since her birth. Cornelia and Cornelis's first child, Rembrandt, was born in 1673. After their second son, Hendric, was born in 1678, Cornelia and her family passed from recorded history. She lives on only here, in the pages of fiction.

Character list from
I Am Rembrandt's Daughter

Rembrandt van Rijn: born in Leiden, July 15, 1606; married Saskia van Uylenburgh, June 22, 1634; died October 4, 1669.

Saskia van Uylenburgh: born August 2, 1612; married Rembrandt van Rijn, June 22, 1634; died June 14, 1642.

Hendrickje Stoffels: born ca. 1626; common-law wife of Rembrandt van Rijn; died ca. July 24, 1663.

Nicolaes Bruyningh: born ca. 1630; died 1680. Merchant.

Cornelia van Rijn: born ca. October 30, 1654, to Hendrickje Stoffels and Rembrandt van Rijn; married painter Cornelis Suythof shortly after May 3, 1670; died Batavia, Dutch East Indies, exact date unknown.

Cornelis Suythof: born ca. 1646; married Cornelia van Rijn shortly after May 3, 1670; died Batavia, Dutch East Indies, after 1689.

Titus van Rijn: born ca. September 22, 1641, to Rembrandt van Rijn and Saskia van Uylenburgh; married Magdalena van Loo, February 28, 1668; died ca. September 7, 1668.

Magdalena van Loo: born ca. May 21, 1642; married Titus van Rijn, February 28, 1668; died ca. October 21, 1669. Related also to Saskia, Hendrick, and Gerrit van Uylenburgh (cousins).

Other children of Rembrandt van Rijn with Saskia:

Rombartus (son): born ca. December 15, 1635; died ca. February 15, 1636.

Cornelia (daughter): born ca. July 22, 1638; died ca. August 13, 1638.

Cornelya (daughter): born ca. July 29, 1640; died ca. August 12, 1640.

Child of Titus van Rijn and Magdalena van Loo:

Titia van Rijn (daughter): born ca. March 22, 1669; died November 22, 1715.

Children of Cornelia van Rijn and Cornelis Suythof:

Rembrandt: born ca. December 5, 1673; date of death unknown.

Hendric: born ca. July 14, 1678; date of death unknown.

Others:

Hendrick van Uylenburgh: art dealer for Rembrandt van Rijn; cousin to Saskia van Uylenburgh (Rembrandt's first wife) and father of Gerrit van Uylenburgh.

Gerrit van Uylenburgh: art dealer, cousin to Saskia van Uylenburgh.

Jan Bruyningh: brother of Nicolaes Bruyningh; father of Carel Bruyningh; merchant.

Carel Bruyningh (*fictitious character*): son of Jan Bruyningh; nephew of Nicolaes Bruyningh; merchant.

Ferdinand Bol: born ca. 1616, died ca. 1680. Student of Rembrandt van Rijn, later a celebrated painter in his own right.

Govert Flinck: born ca. 1615; died ca. 1660. Another student of Rembrandt's who went on to surpass him in popularity in Amsterdam at the time.

Bartholomeus (Bartol) van der Helst: born ca. 1613; died ca. 1670. Contemporary of Rembrandt—most sought out portraitist in the city during Rembrandt's latter years.

Notable Rembrandt Paintings

Family Group. Ca. 1666. Canvas, 126×167 cm. Herzog Anton Ulrich-Museum, Braunschweig.

Titus. Ca. 1658. Canvas, 67.3×55.2 cm. Wallace Collection, London.

Peter Denying Christ. 1660. Canvas, 154×169 cm. Rijksmuseum, Amsterdam.

Two Moors. 1661. Canvas, 77.8×64.4 cm. Mauritshuis, The Hague.

The Sampling Officials. 1662. Canvas, 191.5×279 cm. Rijksmuseum, Amsterdam.

The Oath of Claudius Civilis. Ca. 1661–1662. Canvas, cut down to 196×309 cm. Nationalmuseum, Stockholm.

Self-portrait. Ca. 1661–1662. Canvas, 114.3×95.2 cm. Kenwood House, The Iveagh Bequest, London.

Portrait of Jacob Trip. Ca. 1661. Canvas, 130.5×97 cm. National Gallery, London.

Portrait of Margaretha de Geer. Ca. 1661. Canvas, 130.5×97.5 cm. National Gallery, London.

The Anatomy Lesson of Dr. Jan Deyman. 1656. Canvas, cut down to 100×134 cm. Amsterdams Historisch Museum, Amsterdam.

Juno. Begun about 1661, finished after summer 1665. Canvas, 127×107.5 cm. The Armand Hammer Collection, Los Angeles.

The Evangelist Matthew Inspired by an Angel. 1661. Canvas, 96×81 cm. Musee du Louvre, Paris.

Saskia as Flora. Ca. 1634. Canvas, 125×101 cm. Hermitage, St. Petersburg.

Bathsheba with King David's Letter. 1654. Canvas, 142×142 cm. Louvre, Paris.

Hendrickje at an Open Door. Ca. 1656. Canvas, 88.5×67 cm. Gemäldegalerie, Berlin.

Rembrandt and Saskia in the Scene of the Prodigal Son in the Tavern. 1635. Canvas, 161×131 cm. Gemäldegalerie Alte Meister, Dresden.

Hendrickje. 1660. Canvas, 78.4×68.9 cm. Metropolitan Museum of Art, New York.

Hendrickje Bathing. 1655. Panel, 61.8×47 cm. National Gallery, London.

Officers and Guardsmen of the Amsterdam Civic Guard Company of Captain Frans Banning Cocq (1605–1655): "The Night Watch." 1642. Canvas, 363×437 cm. Rijksmuseum, Amsterdam.

The Jewish Bride. 1667. Canvas, 121.5×166.5 cm. Rijksmuseum, Amsterdam.

Portrait of Nicholas Bruyningh (1629/30–1680). 1652. Canvas, 107.5×91.5 cm. Gemäldegalerie, Kassel.

The Return of the Prodigal Son. Ca. 1668. Canvas, 262×205 cm. Hermitage, St. Petersburg.

LYNN CULLEN is the author of several novels and picture books, including *Moi and Marie Antoinette*. She lives in Atlanta, Georgia. For more information about the author or Rembrandt and his paintings, please visit www.lynncullen.com.

IF YOU ENJOYED

I Am Rembrandt's Daughter . . .

Ophelia
by Lisa Klein

Two Girls of Gettysburg
by Lisa Klein